R. A. Spratt

FRIDAY BARNES
The Plot Thickens

PUFFIN BOOKS

PUFFIN BOOKS

UK | USA | Canada | Ireland | Australia
India | New Zealand | South Africa | China

Penguin Random House Australia is part of the Penguin Random House group of
companies whose addresses can be found at global.penguinrandomhouse.com.

First published by Random House Australia in 2016
This edition published by Puffin Books, an imprint of
Penguin Random House Australia Pty Ltd, in 2020

Cover illustration by Lilly Piri, www.littlegalaxie.com
Cover design by Kirby Armstrong © Penguin Random House Australia Pty Ltd
Internal design and typesetting by Midland Typesetters, Australia

Printed and bound in Australia by Griffin Press, an accredited ISO AS/NZS 14001
Environmental Management Systems printer

 A catalogue record for this
book is available from the
National Library of Australia

ISBN 978 1 76 089215 9 (Paperback)

Penguin Random House Australia uses papers that are natural and recyclable
products, made from wood grown in sustainable forests. The logging and
manufacture processes are expected to conform to the environmental
regulations of the country of origin.

penguin.com.au

Previously in Friday Barnes

As the sun rose over Highcrest Academy the entire student body was enjoying their second, and in some cases third or fourth, helpings of ice-cream. The Headmaster had even decreed that everyone could go back to bed and sleep in for the first two periods of the day, which had made Melanie leap up and kiss him on the cheek. It seemed like the perfect start to a new day on the heels of a very long one.

Ian slid into the seat next to Friday.

'I suppose thanks are in order,' said Ian, with a rueful smile. 'You cleared my name.'

Friday smiled. 'You don't have to thank me. You were my client. I did it for payment.'

'What do you mean?' asked Ian.

'The deal was that I cleared your name and then you owed me a favour,' said Friday. 'That's thanks enough. I'm going to enjoy having that favour up my sleeve.'

'Hang on,' said Ian, starting to get irritated. 'I saved your life. I found you on the cliff face.'

'You fell on me,' said Friday.

'Then shared my jumper with you,' said Ian.

'You did?' said Melanie. 'How romantic. You didn't tell me that, Friday.'

'You didn't bring a mobile phone or any way of attracting the attention of rescuers,' said Friday.

'She's very particular about acts of heroism, isn't she?' Ian said to Melanie.

'She's just feeling vulnerable because you didn't just rescue her physically but emotionally as well,' said Melanie.

'I am not!' said Friday.

'See how red her face is getting?' said Melanie. 'She's embarrassed because I'm speaking the truth.'

Friday stared at her bowl of ice-cream and tried to will her face back to normal colour.

'Oh no!' exclaimed Ian. 'What's going on?!'

Friday looked up to see what had shocked Ian. It was a man she recognised.

'Mr Wainscott?!' exclaimed Friday. 'What are you doing here?'

The last time Friday had seen Ian's father, he'd been yelling abuse at her as he was dragged away by police because she had just proven that he was guilty of bank robbery and insurance fraud. But now Mr Wainscott was completely composed as he calmly made his way across the dining hall, accompanied by a pale, thin man in a grey suit. As he drew close Friday noted that Mr Wainscott was tall, confident and unnervingly handsome, just like Ian.

'I've come to claim custody of my son,' said Mr Wainscott.

Chapter 1

![decorative film strip divider]

Surely Not!

'What's going on here?' demanded the Headmaster as he hurriedly made his way over to the group.

'It's perfectly simple,' said Mr Wainscott, with a condescending smile to the Headmaster. 'I want my boy back.'

'But you're meant to be in jail,' said Friday. 'You were sentenced to six years with a minimum term of three, because you assaulted a police officer while being arrested.'

'I'd hardly call a wedgie an assault,' said Mr Wainscott with a chuckle.

'But you've got two years left on your sentence,' said Friday.

'I have been completely exonerated,' said Mr Wainscott, holding up his hands in a gesture of innocence.

'How can that be?' said Friday. 'You admitted to stealing the diamond.'

'I was under duress,' said Mr Wainscott, with a shake of his head.

'And the diamond was found in the light fitting of your office,' said Friday.

'Planted there by my enemies,' said Mr Wainscott.

'Who would ever believe that?' asked Friday.

'It doesn't matter who believes it,' said Mr Wainscott, a glint in his eye. 'My conviction was overturned on appeal, due to a legal issue.'

'What legal issue?' asked Ian, speaking for the first time.

'The judge was bonkers,' said Mr Wainscott. His eyes crinkled as he smiled. This clearly delighted him.

'It was discovered that Justice Heyton has been

suffering from advanced Alzheimer's disease for some time,' said Mr Wainscott's companion.

Now that she looked at him, Friday realised that it wasn't just the suit, the man was so totally dull that his face seemed grey as well.

'He had been deciding cases based on where his budgerigar did droppings in its cage,' Mr Wainscott's companion continued.

'Who are you?' asked the Headmaster.

'James Archer,' said the dull man. 'I'm Mr Wainscott's lawyer. Here is the court order instructing you to release Ian Wainscott into the custody of his father.' He handed the Headmaster several folded sheets of paper.

The Headmaster flicked through them, quickly scanning each page.

'You can't allow this!' said Friday. 'What about Ian's mother?'

'According to this,' said the Headmaster, 'Mr Wainscott claims that she cannot provide a fit and proper home.'

'There are too many vegetables, but it's not that bad,' said Ian.

'It's not the vegetables that are the problem,' said Mr Wainscott sternly.

'What does that mean?' asked Ian, looking confused.

'You father is alleging that your mother is living with an unsavoury influence,' said the Headmaster as he read further into the document.

'What?' said Ian.

'Oh no,' said Melanie. Being more emotionally intuitive, she was the first to put two and two together.

'Uncle Bernie!' said Friday in realisation.

The Headmaster nodded.

Ian was starting to look very angry. 'So he moved right in as soon as I came back to boarding school. How convenient!'

'This is why she is a poor influence,' said Mr Wainscott with feigned regret. 'Whereas *I* will provide you with a home that is a secure, stable environment.'

'But you're a convicted felon,' protested Friday.

'Not anymore,' said Mr Wainscott smugly. 'Now I am a respectable citizen with a full pardon. Ian is my son, and his place is with his father.'

'But you're the one who sent me to boarding school in the first place,' said Ian, looking confused and hurt.

'And I'm so ashamed of that,' said Mr Wainscott, shaking his head sadly. 'I used to be too career-orientated. But prison made me see the light. It made me appreciate what was truly important – my child. We've lost so much time together, and I want to make up for it. I want you to come home with me right now.'

Ian turned to the Headmaster. 'Do I have to?'

The Headmaster frowned. 'I'm afraid so. The paperwork is all in order, and he is your father.'

'Come with me,' said Mr Wainscott. 'I'm sure the school will be happy to pack up your things and send them on to you.'

'Actually, that's not a service we usually provide,' said the Headmaster.

'I'm sure you'll make an exception,' said Mr Wainscott, with a steely glare. 'It would look terrible in the newspapers if I told them you were with-holding my son's property.'

The Headmaster sighed and muttered to himself, 'Just once I'd like to make it through a day without one of the parents threatening me.'

'Come on, son,' said Mr Wainscott as he smiled at Ian.

Friday noted that Mr Wainscott used the exact same smile Ian used when he was trying to be charming. The supernova smile that made his face radiate handsomeness.

Mr Wainscott's charisma seemed to lock Ian in a tractor beam and pull him forward. Ian took a step towards his dad. Mr Wainscott took Ian's arm above the elbow and started walking quickly with him towards the door.

'Let me see those papers,' said Friday, taking the court order from the Headmaster's hands. She started speed-reading through the pages.

'There's no use,' said the Headmaster. 'You can't ignore a court order. You don't want to end up committing contempt of court. Well, you might, but I don't.'

Friday flicked through to the last page, then looked up. 'We've got to stop them!'

'Why?' asked the Headmaster.

But Friday was already running for the door.

Chapter 2

The Real Reason

As Friday burst out through the ornamental front door of the school, Mr Wainscott was sliding into the driver's seat of his car. Ian and the lawyer were already inside and fastening their safety belts. Friday started running down the front steps. Mr Wainscott started the engine. Friday realised she wasn't going to make it running (not her strength), so she leapt forward, flinging herself onto the bonnet of the car.

1

'Friday! What do you think you are doing?' yelled the Headmaster, who had just burst out of the front doorway himself, alongside Melanie.

'Get her off my car!' yelled Mr Wainscott through the windscreen, so he sounded rather muffled.

'I'm not going anywhere,' said Friday, gripping hold of the windscreen wipers tightly. 'Call the police, Headmaster. This court order is a forgery.'

'It is not!' said Mr Wainscott, getting out of the car. 'Give it to me.' He tried to snatch the court order from Friday, but she pulled it out of the way and stood up on the bonnet so it was out of Mr Wainscott's reach. Ian and Mr Archer got out of the car too.

'How do you know it's a forgery?' asked the Headmaster. 'I've read a few court orders in my time –'

'When the bailiffs come because of your gambling debts?' asked Melanie.

'That's beside the point,' said the Headmaster. 'The point is, that document looked authentic to me.'

'Yes, but the same can't be said for the paper it's printed on,' said Friday.

'Can't you control this girl?' demanded Mr Wainscott.

'Not in the least,' admitted the Headmaster. 'But generally speaking, while she is extremely irritating, she is a force for good.'

'I will sue you for the damage done to my car,' said Mr Wainscott, 'and the slander you're allowing her to commit against me.'

'I don't think you're really going to do that,' said the Headmaster. 'Friday, get down from Mr Wainscott's car and explain what you're talking about.'

'Yes, an explanation would be nice,' said Ian, getting out of the car. 'Is it so hard for you to believe that my father wants me back, just because your father doesn't want to spend time with you?'

'Oooh, that's a really low blow,' said Melanie. 'Don't judge him, Friday. He's only lashing out because he feels vulnerable.'

'Look at the court order. The font is wrong!' said Friday. 'It's printed in Arial. But all government agencies use Calibri as a cost-saving exercise. It uses twenty-three per cent less ink, which equates to a saving of hundreds of thousands of dollars per calendar year.'

'This is ridiculous,' said Mr Wainscott. 'She's clutching at straws.'

'I can prove I'm right,' said Friday. 'Mr Archer, may I borrow your lighter?'

'What?' said the lawyer.

'I can tell from the smoky odour of your suit and yellow-stained fingertips that you are a cigarette smoker,' said Friday. 'May I borrow your lighter?'

Mr Archer held it out to her.

'Did you meet Mr Wainscott in jail?' Friday asked.

Mr Archer flinched. 'Why do you say that?' he asked nervously.

'You are unusually pale and your head is sweaty,' said Friday, 'which suggests you're suffering from vitamin D deficiency from too much time indoors. Add to that the fact that you clearly smoke like a chimney. Not a common habit amongst lawyers, but very common amongst prisoners recently released from a cigarette-free prison.'

'Friday, what are you going to do?' asked the Headmaster.

'Perform a simple test on the paper,' said Friday. She held up the court order, flared up the lighter and set the bottom corner of the document alight.

'Are you out of your mind?!' yelled the Headmaster.

'I'm proving I'm right,' said Friday.

'Ian, get in the car, we're going!' snapped Mr Wainscott.

'No, Dad, I want to hear what she's got to say,' said Ian.

The court order was almost entirely reduced to ashes now. Friday hastily dropped the last burning corner when her fingers got too hot. The remnants of the page were just shrivelled pale-grey ashes on the gravel of the driveway.

'She's mad,' said Mr Wainscott.

'I'm right,' said Friday. 'Look.' She crouched down next to the ashes. 'The ashes are almost white.'

'Friday, none of us understand the significance,' said the Headmaster. 'Explain yourself.'

'This,' said Friday, dramatically whipping another document out of her pocket, 'is a real court order from the Swiss Government forbidding me from ever returning to Switzerland, unless I have a valid passport.'

Friday flicked on the lighter again and set fire to the document. It quickly burned down to a pile of black ash.

'Good gracious,' said the Headmaster. 'She's right. They both looked the same, but their ashes are completely different.'

'It's because of the different carbon content and pH levels,' said Friday. 'Which brings me to the final reason I believe Mr Archer is a former criminal,' said Friday. 'He bears a striking resemblance to D. B. Hatton, who was on the most-wanted list for many years for forging passports.'

Ian turned to confront his father. 'You forged a court order to make me go with you?'

'Yes,' said Mr Wainscott, 'I've missed you, son. I knew I would never get custody through the proper processes. I was desperate.'

'He's lying,' said Melanie.

Everyone turned to look at her.

'Sorry, that sounded really rude,' continued Melanie. 'But I know some people find it hard to tell when a handsome person is lying, especially if they are making eye contact, so I thought I'd point it out so that there's no confusion.'

'Prison changed me, son,' said Mr Wainscott. 'I just want to spend some time with you. Come on, we can go camping, or fishing, or to Disneyland – whatever you want to do.'

Melanie fake-coughed while saying, 'Big fib.'

'I want to believe you,' said Ian.

'But that doesn't mean you have to go with him,' said Friday. 'You're happy here.'

'Am I?' said Ian.

'Well, as happy as a sullen teen can be,' said Friday. 'Tell me, how many times did he write to you from prison?'

'Never,' said Ian.

'Did he send you a birthday card?' asked Friday.

'I'm sorry if the prison shop didn't have a good Hallmark section,' said Mr Wainscott.

'Actually, I know for a fact that prison shops always supply a fully stocked greeting card section because they realise that maintaining family relationships is key to a prisoner's rehabilitation,' said Friday.

'He's my dad, my only dad,' said Ian.

'But ask yourself – why does he want you to go with him?' said Friday.

'You find it impossible to believe that he might want to spend some time with his son?' asked Ian.

'Yes, I do,' said Friday. 'Don't get me wrong, I think you're wonderful . . .'

'Aha!' cried Melanie. 'Finally she admits it.'

'But your father is a classic narcissist,' said Friday.

'He is entirely self-interested. He only cares about what you can do for him.'

'What would that be? Other than be his son?' asked Ian.

'Think about it,' said Friday. 'What does your father have a track record for doing? He hides assets. There was a diamond in his shoe. Then diamonds in Rocky's dog collar.'

'Are you saying my father has hidden something on me?' asked Ian.

'What, like a surgical implant?' asked Melanie.

'Maybe,' said Friday. 'But it would be easier for him to give Ian something that he would always wear and carry with him. Like a watch.'

Ian looked at the watch on his wrist.

'Who gave it to you?' asked Friday.

Ian looked up at his father. 'Dad did, for my eleventh birthday. It's the best present he ever gave me. He had it engraved.'

'So is it a Rolex or something?' asked Melanie. 'Or a turn-of-the-century watch worn by a Russian tsar?'

'It's just an ordinary watch,' said Mr Wainscott. 'Solid Japanese craftsmanship, but nothing to make a fuss about.'

Ian took off his watch and looked it over.

'May I see?' Friday took the watch and held it in her hand. She turned it over. The watch was engraved on the back. It said, *To my son, Ian. Wear this always. Dad.*

'A strange inscription,' said Friday. 'No terms of endearment. No emotional message. Just "wear this".'

'I'm sorry if I haven't got a turn for the sappy phrase,' said Mr Wainscott.

'So it can't be the watch,' said Friday.

'Thank you,' said Mr Wainscott. 'We'll be on our way, then.'

'It must be something inside the watch,' said Friday, with which she took a tiny screwdriver out of her pocket and deftly levered open the back.

'Hey, you'll ruin the waterproof seal!' exclaimed Ian.

'It's okay, I'm sure your father will be able to buy you another with whatever jewels he's got stashed inside,' said Friday as she removed the back, exposing the internal workings. She stared at them for several seconds. Everyone else stared at Friday and the watch for several seconds.

There was nothing to see. Just the simple electronic mechanism of the watch.

'I don't understand,' said Friday.

'What a disgrace,' said Mr Wainscott. 'Hand me that right now so I can have it repaired immediately.'

'I can't believe you broke my watch,' said Ian forlornly.

Friday held out the watch to return it to Mr Wainscott.

'And the backing,' said Mr Wainscott.

Friday looked down and realised she had the backing in her other hand. She turned her hand over and looked at it.

'Stop!' cried Friday. 'Look!'

Inside the back of the watch was a small reddish piece of paper with a black smudge on it.

'Give it to me!' snapped Mr Wainscott, lunging for the watch.

Friday stepped away, and the Headmaster stepped between them. 'I know she's irritating,' said the Headmaster, 'but you can't assault a student.'

'It's just the maker's label,' said Mr Wainscott.

16

'It isn't,' said Friday. She had her jeweller's eyepiece out now so she could inspect it closely.

'Then what is it?' asked Ian.

'The most valuable commodity by weight in the world,' said Friday.

Ian rolled his eyes. 'Great, now she's talking in riddles again.'

'It's a Penny Red,' said Friday. 'A postage stamp.'

'Big deal!' said Ian.

'It is a big deal,' said Friday. 'This is the Holy Grail of stamp collecting.'

'But who cares?' said Ian. 'Stamp collecting is just a hobby for nerds.'

'It is not,' said Friday. 'Okay, well, actually it is. But it is also the single most transportable form of wealth. Stamp collecting is huge in China. The market for collectable stamps has never been stronger. Look at it.' She held up the Penny Red. 'It weighs less than a gram. It looks innocuous. You could hide it anywhere on your person. You could stick it on an envelope and post it to yourself.'

'So what's it worth?' asked Ian.

Friday peered at the stamp again with her jeweller's eyepiece. 'A Penny Red is rare and valuable. But this isn't an ordinary one. It's a plate 77 Penny Red. The plate it was printed with was defective, so after testing, it was destroyed. But one of the test sheets accidentally made it into circulation. There are only nine of these stamps in the world. And the last one to come up for auction sold for £550,000 British sterling.'

'What?!' exclaimed Ian. 'But that's equal to over a million dollars. And I've been wearing it around my wrist all this time.'

'It's brilliant,' said Friday. 'Your watch is water-proof. No harm came to it.'

'But I was wearing a million dollars on my wrist!' said Ian.

'I'll call the police,' said the Headmaster.

'There's no point,' said Friday. 'Mr Wainscott hasn't committed a crime. He just came to get his property back.'

'Being a bad parent isn't a crime,' said Melanie, 'which is lucky for you, Headmaster, because if it was, most of the students here would have their parents in jail, and then there would be no one to pay the school fees.'

'Unless . . . Mr Wainscott stole the Penny Red. After all, he did get a degree from Barnum and

Bailey's Circus Skills University with a minor in sleight of hand. So did you?' asked Friday, turning to Mr Wainscott. 'It would be easy enough to find out. So few of these exist.'

'I acquired it perfectly legally,' said Mr Wainscott.

'Let me guess, not by paying market value at a reputable auction?' as Friday.

'I won it in a high stakes mahjong game at a Macau casino,' said Mr Wainscott. He couldn't stop himself from smirking with pride.

Friday handed the watch to Mr Wainscott. 'Here, this is what you want, isn't it?'

Mr Wainscott took the watch. 'I would say "thank you", but I can't think of any earthly reason why I should be polite to you.' He opened the door of the car. Mr Archer got in on the passenger side.

'What about me?' asked Ian.

'What about you?' asked Mr Wainscott.

'Don't you want me . . . to come with you?' asked Ian.

Mr Wainscott sighed. 'Of course I do, but things are going to be very busy for a while. I've got to get the business up and running again. I need to spend some time in the Cayman Islands.'

'I'd love to visit the Cayman Islands,' said Ian.

'You'll be better off here,' said Mr Wainscott. 'When I'm back on top, I'll come for you.'

'How long will that take?' asked Ian.

'Three months, at most,' said Mr Wainscott. He shut the door of his car and pulled away.

Ian watched his father drive off. Everyone was silent for a moment, not knowing what to say. Eventually Friday stepped forward and touched Ian's arm.

'Are you okay?' she asked.

'No, I'm not!' yelled Ian, swivelling to turn his fury on Friday. 'How could you? You just had to grind in every last grain of humiliation, didn't you? My father doesn't want me. My own father tricks me into hiding his money, the same way he hid his money on his dog. Well, thank you, thank you very much for totally humiliating me and ruining my life.'

Friday was sure Ian was about to cry. She was pretty sure she was about to cry herself. But Ian stormed off before either one of them could start the waterworks.

'Are you okay?' asked Melanie.

'No,' said Friday, then she couldn't hold it in any longer. She burst into tears.

Chapter 3

A New Teacher

The following weeks were not a fun time at Highcrest Academy. Ian had apparently, in his mind at least, declared war on Friday. Every couple of days she was met with a new and original prank. Like the fire sprinklers going off, but only above her desk in the biology lab. Or all her clothes coming back from the laundry dyed brown, so now everything she wore matched her brown cardigans. Or the lock on her dorm room changing so that she couldn't get out and had to climb through the second-storey window, only to discover that an all-school fire drill had been called on the lawn directly outside.

'I'm thinking of applying to university again,' said Friday, as she and Melanie walked towards the school hall. It was time for the weekly assembly.

'I thought you said they wouldn't take you because you were too young?' said Melanie.

'They did say that,' agreed Friday, 'but I suspect that was just the excuse they used because the Vice Chancellor found me annoying during my interview when I told him that the statistical analysis in his PhD thesis was based on a false premise.'

'Yes, that can't have helped.' Melanie nodded.

They started shuffling into the hall with the other students, trying to find seats behind someone tall so that the teachers on stage couldn't see them.

'But maybe if I try another university,' said Friday. 'And I only say nice, positive things like . . . well, I can't think of any, but you could write up a list for me to memorise.'

'Like, "That's a nice tie you're wearing"?' said Melanie.

'Perfect,' said Friday. 'It would never occur to me to say that.'

'But why is it you want to leave?' asked Melanie.

'The pranks,' said Friday. 'Ian's wearing me down. Being drenched or locked out is bad enough, but the waves of hate I can feel emanating from him every time we're in the same room are exhausting.'

'You're so in tune with his emotions,' said Melanie. 'Why don't you prank him back? I believe that is what high-spirited teenagers are meant to do.'

'I'm only twelve,' said Friday. 'Besides, I kind of deserve all the pranking. I was insensitive. And I have ruined his relationship with his father.'

'I'm sure he'll move on eventually,' said Melanie. 'Although literature does not back up my theory. You are the love of his life, so it may take a while.'

The music began to play and the students fell silent as the Headmaster led the parade of teachers into the hall. The heads of department always had to don their academic robes for this ritual.

'Who's that?' asked Friday.

At the back of the group was a man wearing normal clothes: a blue-collared shirt and tan chinos. But he stood out because his clothes were amazingly creased.

'How do you even get clothes that scrumpled?' asked Melanie.

'I don't know,' said Friday.

'Really? Because the only other person I've ever seen looking that scrumpled is you,' said Melanie.

'I just don't iron them,' said Friday. 'I don't actively go out of my way to scrunch them up.'

'Are you sure?' said Melanie. 'Because I've seen you put on a pair of jeans you found screwed up in a ball behind your mattress.'

Friday noticed there was a covered easel up on the stage. 'I wonder what that is?' she said.

The teachers were now finding their seats on the stage and the music stopped. The Headmaster walked over to the microphone. 'Good morning,' he said with a jolly smile.

'He's in a fine mood,' said Melanie. 'Usually he yells at someone before he gets started.'

'It has recently been drawn to my attention that there is a morale problem here at Highcrest,' said the Headmaster.

Melanie nudged Friday. 'He's talking about you.'

Friday scowled. She wasn't in a fine mood.

'So I cast my mind to the idea of what could

energise this school academically,' said the Headmaster.

'Chocolate pudding!' called Patel.

'Patel, detention!' snapped the Headmaster. 'One week, an hour a day.'

Patel visibly deflated. His joke had not been funny enough to warrant this level of backlash.

'Where was I?' said the Headmaster. 'I have decided to inspire you with an eight-week intensive art program. Creative thinking is, I'm told, important in any number of professions. It certainly is in insider trading, which is what so many of the students at this school seem to go on to do. But aside from that, an exploration of the arts should open your minds to a world of creative possibilities, which will hopefully improve your education and cheer you all up so I don't get so many notes whining about what Mrs Marigold has been cooking for dinner. Luckily for you, I have been able to hire the finest talent in this field.'

The Headmaster gestured towards the crumpled man as he slouched in his chair. If body language had volume, his was shouting how bored he was with the whole proceeding.

Now that Friday looked at him front on, her eyes were not drawn to his clothes. They were drawn to his face. He was very, very handsome. He had a strong jaw, straight nose and faded auburn hair that looked like he had forgotten to have it cut for three months. His face was extremely freckled, so much so that it almost looked like a deep suntan, and he was more wrinkled than a man his age would usually be. But somehow his wrinkles made him seem rugged and handsome.

'It's wrong to objectify a teacher,' whispered Melanie.

'What?' asked Friday.

'You're thinking about how handsome he is, aren't you?' said Melanie.

'I was only making empirical observations,' said Friday.

'Hmm,' said Melanie. 'Just so long as the empirical observations don't get out of hand.'

'Let me introduce you to . . .' said the Headmaster '. . . Mr Lysander Brecht.'

There was a cacophony of gasps from the student body. Mr Brecht inspected his fingernails as if they were the most fascinating things he had ever seen.

'Who?' asked Friday.

'He's one of the most famous contemporary artists in the world,' said Melanie. 'He won the Armstead Portrait Prize for his picture of himself as a nineteenth-century Russian peasant woman.'

Friday looked at Mr Brecht. He was the embodiment of masculinity. 'Surely it wasn't a self-portrait, then?'

'Oh no, he looked very good ankle-deep in mud, wearing a blue dress and headscarf,' said Melanie. 'You could really see into his soul.'

'But if he is such a great artist, why on earth would he come and teach here?' said Friday. She watched Mr Brecht. He looked lethargic, but Friday suspected it was a deceptive lethargy, like that of an African lion right before it leaps up and rips a zebra's head off.

'That is a mystery,' said Melanie.

Friday smiled. That's just what she needed – a good mystery to dust off the cobwebs. Her neurons were already starting to fire up in anticipation. Her headache was clearing. It seemed that in her case, at least, the Headmaster's plan to cheer up the student body was working.

'Of course, it might have something to do with the massive fine he got from the tax department for tax evasion,' added Melanie.

'I didn't read about that in the paper,' said Friday.

'Really?' said Melanie. 'It was in all the gossip magazines.'

'It is also our great honour,' continued the Headmaster, 'to have Mr Brecht's most famous masterpiece, "The Red Princess", on display here for the duration of the visit.' The Headmaster turned to the curtain-covered easel. 'Mr Brecht, if you'll do the honours.'

Mr Brecht rolled his eyes. He begrudgingly stood up, grabbed the corner of the curtain and whipped it off the easel.

The entire school gasped. There was no painting. Just a timber frame.

'Is it meant to be an empty frame?' Friday whispered to Melanie.

'No, it's meant to be a famous picture of a baby with red hair nestled in a reed basket,' whispered Melanie.

'Where's my picture?' bellowed Mr Brecht, turning on the Headmaster. He might've looked scruffy but he had a very posh voice. And a very loud one too.

'It was right there, just before assembly,' spluttered the Headmaster.

'That painting is worth millions of dollars!' exclaimed Mr Brecht.

'Who did this?' demanded the Headmaster, turning on the student body.

All the students sat incredibly still, knowing that with the Headmaster this angry, the slightest body movement could be taken as an admission of guilt.

'I will get to the bottom of this,' declared the Headmaster. 'And when I do, the perpetrator will be expelled!'

'They'll go to jail!' added Mr Brecht.

'That too,' agreed the Headmaster.

Chapter 4

Too Far

All day long the school was abuzz with gossip and speculation about the missing 'Red Princess'. Friday was very intrigued by the mystery herself. But she didn't get a chance to have a good hard think about it because every five minutes someone was coming up and asking her opinion. She needed somewhere nice and quiet. So she decided to spend the afternoon in study hall.

Highcrest Academy had a large study hall, where

students could go and work quietly at any time. It was full of tables and chairs and reading lights. And there were usually very few people in it, especially on a sunny day.

Melanie went with Friday because she had found that if she pushed two armchairs over to a window they made a lovely sunny bed, so she could enjoy all the benefits of taking a nap in the sunshine without any of the risk of being hit by a stray football.

But on this day they were to be thwarted. When Friday and Melanie walked over to study hall after lunch, there was a large sign stuck to the door:

Closed for renovation
For quiet study, use the picnic tables by the swamp

'Urgh,' said Melanie. 'We've got to walk all the way down there.'

'I do hope that by "renovation" they don't mean they're turning the study hall into a computer lab,' said Friday.

'I thought you liked computers,' said Melanie.

'I do,' said Friday, 'but computers are everywhere, whereas a quiet space is incredibly hard to find.'

The girls ambled towards the swamp.

'I just hope they've moved some armchairs down there,' said Melanie. 'Picnic tables are all very well for sitting, but it's hard to lie on one.'

'At least it's near the swamp,' said Friday. 'I'm sure you can find a mossy patch of ground that is quite comfortable.'

When they arrived at the outdoor study area, there were four picnic tables to choose between. But three of the picnic tables had signs on them saying:

Wet Paint

'That's not very well-organised,' said Melanie, 'to close the study hall, and paint the outdoor study area on the same day.'

'It probably wasn't arranged by the same people,' said Friday. 'The caretaker, Mr Pilcher, would paint the outdoor tables, whereas the Headmaster would arrange tradesmen to renovate the study hall.'

The girls sat down and started to get their books out.

'Barnes!'

Friday turned to see, Parker, a year 9 boy, walking towards her.

'Friday,' said Friday.

'No, I think you'll find it's *Monday*,' said Parker.

'My name is Friday,' said Friday. 'Please stop calling me Barnes all the time.'

'Oh, sorry, Barnes,' said Parker. 'Won't interrupt you for too long. The Headmaster has got me showing this new boy around, thought I should introduce him to you in case he gets himself into any trouble.'

Friday looked at the new boy. He was very tall, at least six feet, and thin. But his most distinctive feature was his sense of style. He wore all black, and his hair was black with blue spikey tips. In contrast, his face was an almost sickly pale white.

'Are you wearing eye make-up?' asked Melanie, as she peered at the boy. 'Sorry, I shouldn't have said that, it was thoughtless. Clearly, you are wearing eye make-up. What I should have said was, "Why are you wearing eye make-up?" but that's none of my business, so just ignore me.'

The boy did not respond, except to turn red in the face.

Parker was also staring at his eyes now, Melanie's revelation having made him forget entirely about his reason for being there.

'You were going to introduce us,' Friday prompted him.

'What? Oh yes!' said Parker, finally managing to tear his gaze away. 'This is Epstein. He's a new boy. He's going into year 8.'

'Nice to meet you, Epstein,' said Friday. 'Do you have a first name? Parker struggles to remember more than one name per person.'

'Epstein *is* his first name!' said Parker triumphantly. 'His surname is Smith.'

'*Smythe*,' said Epstein, speaking for the first time.

'Are you sure?' asked Parker. 'You're not pulling my leg, are you? I'm terrible at knowing when people are doing that.'

'Why are you changing schools so late in the academic year?' asked Friday.

'Friday, I know you like me to point out when you are being socially inappropriate,' said Melanie. 'This is one of those times. He might not want to tell us if he got expelled from his previous school.'

'You just made inappropriate comments about his eye make-up,' said Friday. 'Why can't I ask a perfectly innocent question about his schooling?'

'My father got a new job so we had to move,' said Epstein.

'What does your father do?' asked Friday.

'Not much,' said Epstein. 'Fraud, mainly.'

'That's what a lot of the parents here do,' said Melanie with a smile. 'You should have no trouble fitting in.'

Epstein didn't smile back. He didn't frown, either. He just looked blankly at the two girls, then dropped his gaze to his feet.

'All right,' said Parker. 'We'd better keep moving. I've got to show Epstein where all the lavatories are. I remember what it's like to be new. It's fine if you get confused trying to find a classroom, but things can go horribly wrong if you can't locate a toilet.'

The boys turned and walked away. Melanie lay down the length of one of the bench seats with her head rested on a maths textbook. Friday opened her book. She was reading a copy of *The Chemistry of Paint and Painting*. Friday was finding the chapter on pigments to be particularly fascinating, so she didn't notice when the picnic table she was sitting at started to move.

'What's happening?' said Melanie, as she swung up into the seated position.

Friday looked up to see the trees move or, as her brain soon processed, she was actually moving relative to the trees. Friday bent over and looked under the table. There was a small electric motor bolted to the underside, with cables running down each table leg. Friday leaned over further and saw what she had failed to notice when she first sat down.

'Someone has embedded wheels in the legs of this table!' said Friday. 'And there is a one-thousand-kilowatt engine powering them.'

At that moment the table started to accelerate. It was heading straight for the pier that reached out over the swamp.

'Jump!' Friday yelled at Melanie.

'But I don't like exercise!' said Melanie.

'Jump off now!' said Friday. 'Or in a few seconds you'll be swimming.'

Melanie disliked swimming more than jumping. Not that swimming wasn't pleasant, but because it required washing your hair afterwards. She spun her feet out from under the table, ready to leap clear but then she hesitated. The table had picked up speed.

'Jump!' cried Friday.

'I'm not sure about this,' said Melanie.

But the decision was made for her. The picnic table hit a rock and Melanie fell off. Friday turned to see that her friend was all right. Melanie rolled into the fall and sat up, apparently unscathed.

Friday spun around the other way to jump off herself; she only had a second before the table was going to drive onto the pier. Friday gripped the edge of her seat, braced her foot against the diagonal leg of the table and pushed to leap off. But she didn't go anywhere. Something was holding her to the table. Friday looked down to see a long strand of her cardigan caught in a crack in the bench seat. She grabbed her cardigan and tried to yank it free, but the polyester wool blend was surprisingly strong. She was stuck. The table was rattling down the pier now.

Friday was starting to panic. She yanked her cardigan again, but it didn't work.

'Take it off!'

Friday turned back to the bank. Melanie was yelling at her, 'Take it off!'

Friday quickly tried to undo the buttons on her cardigan. But the adrenalin that was now pumping through her veins was making her hands shake.

'Take it off!' yelled Melanie again.

Friday looked up to see the end of the pier just a few metres away. She grabbed the hem of her cardigan and pulled it over her head. But with the strand still snagged on the bench, this pulled her head down more than it pulled the cardigan up. So Friday's head was entangled in her knitwear, with her face just inches from the bench, when the whole picnic table drove straight off the edge of the pier and splashed into the water. As the table dropped down, inertia pulled Friday's head up, so when the table hit the water, momentum slammed her forehead into the hardwood beam.

As the splash receded, the picnic table was adrift in the middle of the swamp, with Friday floating off to the side, her cardigan-wrapped head slumped on the bench seat.

'Friday!' cried Melanie. 'Wake up!'

That's when the table started to sink. Timber is obviously buoyant, but when attached to a metal frame and a heavy engine, it is substantially less so.

The end farthest from Friday's head began to tip up, which meant the end with Friday's head began to sink down.

'No!' cried Melanie, as she sprinted down the pier (the first time she had run anywhere in several years), but she was soon passed by someone moving a lot faster. It was the boy in black, Epstein. As he ran down the pier he whipped his black shirt off over his head, revealing a surprisingly athletic if somewhat slim figure, and he gracefully dived straight off the end, reaching Friday in three perfect freestyle strokes. He untangled her from the cardigan just as the picnic table disappeared under the water, grasped her firmly by the arms and swam sidestroke with her back to the pier.

There was a ladder at the end so Melanie, with the help of Parker who had also run to them, soon pulled Friday out while Epstein clambered up onto the decking.

'Is she okay?' asked Epstein.

Friday coughed and spluttered, pulling herself into a sitting position. 'Yeah, I'm fine,' said Friday. 'Just a bump on the head.' She rubbed a lump on her forehead.

'And you nearly drowned,' said Melanie.

'I just swallowed a little water,' said Friday huskily as she coughed some more.

She looked up at Epstein. He was tall when she first met him, but now that she was sitting down and he was standing over her, he seemed very tall indeed. She met his eyes and said, 'Thank you.' She would have liked to have said more but then she had a coughing fit.

'Are you all right?' Melanie asked Epstein.

'Fine,' said Epstein. Clearly the short swim had barely taxed his cardiovascular system.

'It's just that there is black stuff running down your forehead,' said Melanie. 'So I wondered if you'd had some sort of head injury, too.'

Epstein ran his hand across his forehead. His fingers came away black. He blushed.

'It's hair dye,' said Friday. 'Epstein is a redhead.'

'How do you know?' asked Epstein.

'Armpits,' said Friday, pointing at Epstein's armpits.

Now Epstein practically blushed purple.

'Don't tell anyone,' said Epstein.

'Why not?' asked Melanie. 'Being a redhead isn't

so bad . . . Obviously you can never go out in the sun without burning to a crisp, and people do say that redheads have terrible tempers, and it's hard to find shirts in a colour that really suits you. But, apart from that, there's almost no universal social stigma.'

'I got teased a lot at my old school,' said Epstein. 'I'd appreciate it if you didn't mention it.'

'You saved my life,' said Friday, coughing up some swamp water. 'Keeping quiet is the least I can do.'

They were interrupted by thundering footsteps running down the pier.

Friday looked up to see Ian sprinting towards her. He came to a skidding halt, panting heavily as he struggled to get air into his lungs.

'Are you okay?' he asked.

'I thought you weren't talking to Friday,' said Melanie. 'Oh, I see, losing her made you realise your true feelings for her.'

'No, he's just feeling guilty,' said Friday.

Now Ian blushed, although it was hard to tell whether it was with shame or anger.

'You're the one who put the motor on the picnic table, aren't you?' asked Friday.

'I'm not admitting anything,' said Ian stubbornly.

'What's that in your pocket?' Friday pointed at a large lumpy bulge in Ian's hoodie. 'It's a remote control, isn't it? Let me guess, you were someplace where you'd have the perfect alibi for this prank. Was it choir rehearsal? Cricket practice?'

'He was in detention,' said Parker. 'I saw him when I was showing Epstein around the school.'

'Perfect,' said Friday. 'Detention is in maths classroom one – which is on the second floor of the science block, which would give you a perfect view of the swamp. You could control the whole fiasco from up there, and if anyone suspected you, you could say you were under close watch in detention. But it all went wrong, didn't it?'

'Why didn't you just jump free?' asked Ian.

'Her cardigan got caught,' said Melanie.

'Those stupid, ugly cardigans!' said Ian.

'The cardigan is just an ordinary cardigan,' said Friday.

'That is extraordinarily ugly,' said Melanie.

'It's the motorised picnic table doing speeds of forty kilometres per hour that was the problem,' said Friday. 'A problem *you* caused.'

'It was just a prank,' said Ian.

'You've gone too far,' said Friday. 'It's not my fault your dad is a self-absorbed conman who hides postage stamps in your watch.'

'You didn't have to make such a public spectacle of finding out,' said Ian.

'But I didn't deserve this!' said Friday, pointing to the lump on her forehead. 'I just stopped your father from serving a forged court document. I don't deserve to be drowned in a swamp as punishment.'

'It was an accident,' said Ian.

'No, it was a nasty, dangerous prank that you didn't think through,' said Friday. 'If my cardigan hadn't been caught, you'd be sitting up in detention chortling away to yourself right now.'

'Actually, chortling isn't allowed in detention,' said Parker. 'I know, because I got an extra week of detention for doing it once.'

'Stay away from me,' Friday said, stabbing her finger into Ian's chest. 'I won't be your punching bag anymore.'

Friday turned and started sloshing back along the pier. It was hard to tell if the water running down her face was swamp water, or tears, or a combination of both.

Chapter 5

▗▞▚▞▚▞▚▞▚▞▚▞▚▞▚▞▚▚

Stuck

The Headmaster was still preoccupied with the elusive 'Red Princess'. He had launched a full search of the school in an effort to find the missing painting. But he hadn't got very far before the students' lawyers became involved, and he'd had to go before a magistrate to justify why he'd damaged Tabitha Cooper's Taylor Swift poster. The corner had torn when the Headmaster had detached the sticky tack to look behind the poster. The magistrate had not been sympathetic to the Headmaster's argument that he thought there might be a multi-million-dollar painting hidden behind it.

Things were fairly quiet for the next few days. Ian had been sent on a cricket camp with the rest of the first 11. So Friday was having a pleasant holiday from his sarcasm and pranks.

Friday and Melanie were idly wandering back to their dorm room after the last lesson of the day, when a huge boy called Dexter came chasing after them.

'Melly, Friday!' called Dexter.

'What is it?' asked Melanie. Dexter was a good friend of her brother Binky, so she knew him well.

'It's Binky,' said Dexter. 'He's stuck.'

'Really?' said Melanie. 'In what? I hope it's not the mud in the swamp. I love my brother, but there are some things I just don't want to do, and ruining my shoes is one of them.'

'He's stuck in the vending machine,' said Dexter.

'Surely, he's too large?' said Friday. Binky was now six foot five and very big and muscly.

'Just his arm,' said Dexter. 'But his arm's attached to the rest of him, so he can't go anywhere. He's going to be in trouble if one of the teachers catches him like that.'

'We'd better come and see what we can do,' said Friday.

Melanie and Friday followed Dexter to the vending machine in the stairwell of the English department. It was tucked in behind the staircase, so it wasn't visible unless you walked right around, planning to buy a snack.

As they rounded the balustrade, they saw the first indication of the predicament – Binky's legs. His legs were long, thick tree trunks at the best of times, but now that he was forced to half-lie on the floor they seemed to sprawl out for miles. When Friday and Melanie stood in front of the vending machine, Binky was a sorry sight. His right arm was stuck in the release tray at the bottom, his left arm holding his torso off the ground. It looked very uncomfortable.

'Hello Melly,' said Binky cheerfully. 'I'm so glad to see you.'

'What happened?' asked Melanie. 'Were you stealing a chocolate bar?'

'Gosh, no,' said Binky. 'But that's why I sent Dexter to find you. I know it looks that way. I don't want a member of staff to catch me red-handed. Or red-armed.'

'Then why is your arm stuck in a vending machine?' asked Friday.

'He was hungry,' explained Dexter.

'I don't follow,' said Friday.

'I always get a chocolate bar from this vending machine every morning after first period,' said Binky defensively. 'The rugby master has me on a weights program before school and I get really, really hungry.'

'Binky!' exclaimed Melanie. 'That doesn't make stealing all right.'

'But it wasn't stealing,' argued Binky. 'I put in my money. The machine just didn't give me a chocolate bar. Really, it stole from me!'

'So you decided to take the law into your own hands?' asked Friday.

'I didn't think it would be this difficult,' said Binky. 'The chocolate bar looked so close. I thought I'd easily be able to reach it.'

Friday peered into the machine. She could see the problem. Binky's arm had twisted up inside the machine successfully, but in his attempt to reach the Mars Bar, his cuff had become caught on the spiral that held the chocolate bars upright.

'Well, you are only millimetres away,' said Friday. 'But you're snagged on the spiral of the screw conveyor.'

'The what?' asked Binky. 'That sounds painful.'

'No, it's just a simple screw,' said Friday. 'A coil, really. It works on the same principle as an Archimedes' screw. The screw will push things forward without actually moving forward itself.'

'Still don't follow,' said Binky.

'It's a simple but brilliant piece of technology that an old Greek guy thought up two thousand years ago,' said Friday. 'He came up with it as a way to irrigate the plains of Egypt. And now vending machine manufacturers use it as a way of distributing candy bars.'

'That's progress,' said Melanie.

'Since it's just your cuff that is caught,' said Friday, 'can't you pull your arm free? The material should tear off.'

'I've tried,' said Binky. 'I'm stuck in too awkward a position. I can't pull on it with enough force.'

'We'll have to get you out another way, then,' said Friday.

'Do you want me to smash the glass?' asked Dexter.

'No,' said Friday. 'Being wrongly accused of stealing a chocolate bar pales in comparison to being rightly accused of smashing a vending machine.'

'You can't just leave me here!' said Binky. 'Someone's bound to notice. And if I'm caught with my arm in a vending machine, the Headmaster will sack me as a prefect.'

'That would be a shame. But it is a miracle that you've been a prefect for months and he hasn't sacked you already,' said Melanie.

'True,' conceded Binky.

'I think I can get you out,' said Friday. 'How much money do you have?'

'Friday!' exclaimed Melanie. 'This is my brother you're talking about. Are you really going to force him to pay you for your help?'

'She should,' said Binky. 'I get in to trouble often enough. I like to know Friday is there to help me out.'

'I'm not going to charge Binky,' said Friday. 'I need money for the vending machine.'

'I hardly think now is a good time to be eating chocolate,' said Melanie.

'Just give me your change and I'll show you,' said Friday.

Melanie and Dexter handed over all the loose change from their pockets. It came to a total of $3.10.

'I need another forty cents,' said Friday.

'You can get a milk chocolate bar for that,' said Melanie.

'Yes, but I need a Mars Bar,' said Friday.

'I've got some coins,' said Binky, 'but they're in my right pocket and I can't reach them.'

'I'll get it,' said Friday. She stepped over Binky so that one foot was balanced between his legs and the other was wedged against the vending machine. Then she bent over to reach into Binky's pocket. Her face was jammed up against Binky's shoulder and her hair was right in his face. He sneezed.

'Achoo!' said Binky. 'Sorry, the feather in your pork-pie hat tickled my nose.'

It was hard getting her fingers into Binky's pocket because the way he was sitting was holding the material closed. She pressed forward, trying to reach her fingers in. She felt the warm metal against her fingertips when a sudden noise made her flinch.

'Hello, what's this then?' asked Ian.

Friday tried to look up, but that made her lose her balance and topple onto Binky.

'Hello Wainscott,' said Binky. 'I don't suppose we could borrow forty cents, could we?'

Ian fished the money out of his pocket and handed it to Binky, who handed it to Friday.

'Payment for another case well done?' asked Ian.

Friday just glared at Ian. 'Hardly. What are you doing here? I thought you were at cricket camp.'

'Been counting the days, have you?' Ian smirked. 'We came back a day early because of the rain.'

'It's not raining,' noted Melanie.

'It was when someone rigged the sprinklers so they couldn't be turned off.' Ian winked.

Friday got up, fed the money into the vending machine, and then punched in two numbers on the keypad.

'What are you doing?' asked Binky, alarmed that Friday was operating the machine in which his arm was trapped.

The money rattled down, and the machine started to whirr and hiss pneumatically.

'Owww!' cried Binky. 'It's breaking my arm.'

The coil that Binky's cuff was caught on started to turn.

'Stay calm,' said Friday.

'Easy for you to say!' yelled Binky. 'It isn't *your* arm.'

'Stand back!' yelled Ian. Friday turned to see him grab the fire extinguisher off the wall.

'What are you doing?' demanded Friday.

'Saving Binky's arm,' said Ian. He held up the fire extinguisher and started to swing it at the glass.

'Nooo!' cried Friday, jumping in front of the fire extinguisher.

Ian tried to stop the swing, but he only slowed it. The fire extinguisher banged into Friday, who banged into the vending machine. It caught her in the solar plexis, knocking the breath out of her, and she slumped to the ground.

'Are you okay?' asked Ian.

'Urrgh,' moaned Friday.

'Here, have a Mars Bar,' said Binky.

Friday looked up to see Binky holding out the chocolate bar.

'It worked,' said Friday with a smile.

Binky looked at his arm. 'Yes, it did. The machine just tore the cuff button off.'

'I knew it would,' said Friday. 'The screw conveyor had enough power to move the button, but not your arm. So the button had to give way.'

Melanie reached into the release tray. 'Here's the button.'

'Mmmm-mm,' said Binky. He couldn't say anything more eloquent because he was eating the chocolate bar.

'The really intriguing question here is,' said Friday, as she peered into the workings of the vending machine at the back, 'why would anyone want to trap Binky's arm in a vending machine?'

'There always has to be a conspiracy with you, hasn't there?' said Ian. 'It's simple – Binky was hungry, the machine didn't work properly, he stuck his arm into the machine. No offence, Binky, but it's not like this sort of thing is wildly out of character for you.'

'No offence taken,' said Binky. 'You're entirely right. I got my foot stuck in a storm water drain last week when I tried getting a soccer ball out. This sort of thing happens to me all the time.'

'But if someone did want to delay Binky for some reason,' said Friday, 'this would be perfect. He always uses the same vending machine, at the same time, to get the same chocolate bar. All you'd have to do is stick a lump of Blu-Tack in the vending machine so that when the spiral turned forward the chocolate bar wouldn't fall.'

Friday put her foot in the dispenser tray.

'You're not going to stick your leg in there, are you?' asked Melanie.

'No, I'm just going to have a look,' said Friday. She hoisted herself up so she could look down on the shelf that the chocolate bar had come from. 'Intriguing.'

'What is it?' asked Melanie.

'It's not a lump of Blu-Tack,' said Friday. 'It's a lump of clay. Like the type we use in art class.'

Friday climbed down from the vending machine.

'The next question is – what's the motive?' said Friday. 'Binky, where should you be right now?'

'I've got a free period,' said Binky, 'so I normally go back to my room to study.'

'You mean take a nap, don't you?' said Melanie.

Binky blushed. 'You're not the only one who likes napping, you know.'

'I know,' said Melanie. 'That's how I know it's what you really want to do.'

'So perhaps the motive for trapping Binky in the vending machine,' said Friday, 'was really to keep him from going back to his room.'

'What could be going on in my room?' asked Binky. 'I hope they haven't mussed up my clothes. I spent hours doing my ironing last night.'

'There's only one way to find out,' said Friday. 'Let's take a look.'

Chapter 6

▬▬▬▬▬▬▬▬▬▬▬▬

Binky's Room

Friday, Melanie and Ian went with Binky back to his room. (Dexter had to go to his physics lesson, because his teacher threw whiteboard markers at late people.) When they arrived, the first thing Friday noticed was that the door was unlocked.

'It's clearly been picked by an expert,' said Friday, as she peered closely at the lock. 'There are no scratches around the chamber.'

'That's more likely to be because I never lock it,' confessed Binky.

'What?' said Friday.

'Well, I play so much sport I'm forever taking my clothes on and off,' explained Binky.

'Binky!' exclaimed Melanie. 'Don't be disgusting.'

'It's true,' said Binky. 'And every time I get changed, I always forget to swap things over from my pockets. I kept getting locked out. I found it was much easier just to never lock the door at all.'

'But don't people steal things out of your room?' asked Ian.

'Oh yes,' said Binky. 'But only things like pens, tennis balls and sneakers. It's not a big deal.'

Friday tentatively pushed the door open. Binky's room was immaculate.

'Has someone broken in and tidied everything?' asked Friday. No one in her family had ever valued tidiness. It was a foreign condition to her.

'Oh no, this is how it always looks,' said Binky. 'You've got to be organised and tidy when you've got a mind like a sieve, otherwise you end up in all sorts of muddles.'

Friday looked about. There was absolutely nothing out of place. She wasn't sure where to start. All of Binky's books and stationery sat in ordered piles on his desk. His clothes were neatly hung or stacked in his wardrobe. Even his sporting equipment was perfectly cleaned and lined up along the wall, waiting for its next use. Unlike other boys, Binky did not have any posters of sports teams or pop stars on his walls. He just had one framed Monet print of a field full of wild flowers. Friday had seen the same print many times before in hospitals and motel rooms.

'Did you pick this picture?' Friday asked Binky.

'Gosh, no,' said Binky. 'Don't know much about art. It seemed nice and cheerful, though, so I didn't want to offend anyone by changing it.'

Friday peered closer. The picture was exactly straight, but there was an arch-shaped scuff mark near one of the bottom corners.

'When did you last straighten the picture?' asked Friday.

'I never have,' said Binky. 'It's always seemed perfectly level to me.'

'But there's this scuff mark near the corner,' said Friday. 'It's the same colour as the frame. It's the type of mark you make when you straighten a picture and leave a little scrape on the paintwork on the wall.'

'So there is,' said Binky.

'Was the mark there before?' asked Friday.

Binky peered at it. Friday didn't really expect him to know. Binky was as vague as Melanie, in his own unique way.

'No, it wasn't,' said Binky, with surprising decisiveness. 'I would have fixed it up if it was like that before. It would be easy enough to clean off.' Binky leaned forward to rub the mark with his thumb.

Friday grabbed his hand to stop him. 'No, don't do that,' said Friday. 'It's evidence.'

'Of what?' asked Ian.

'Let's see,' said Friday. She carefully reached out with two hands and lifted the picture off the wall. There were no other marks on the wall behind it.

'Nothing,' said Binky.

'Not on the wall,' agreed Friday. 'But maybe here.' She flipped the picture over in her hand and was shocked by her discovery.

'"The Red Princess"!' exclaimed Melanie.

Lysander Brecht's famous masterpiece was sticky-taped to the back of Binky's print.

Binky went pale. 'I didn't put it there!'

'Of course you didn't,' said Friday. 'Someone tricked you into getting your arm caught in a vending machine so that they could put it here. The question is – who?'

'And why?' said Ian.

Friday looked closer at the painting. 'This isn't right.'

'What do you mean?' asked Ian.

'It's called "The Red Princess",' said Friday, 'because the baby princess has red hair. Her hair is black here. Someone has painted over it.' She dabbed the hair on the baby's head. 'The paint is still tacky to touch.'

'Who would do that?' asked Ian.

'This crime is getting stranger and stranger,' said Friday. 'And there's something odd about the face of the baby . . .'

Binky looked over Friday's shoulder. 'I don't see what the fuss is about, anyway. I'd rather look at the picture on the other side with all the flowers.'

'We'll have to take this to the Headmaster,' said Friday. 'It will be interesting to see what Mr Brecht has to say about someone painting over his great masterpiece.'

Suddenly they heard a loud thud and a muffled cry of 'Ow!'.

'What was that?' asked Melanie.

'It sounded like it came from next door,' said Binky.

Friday was not asking questions. She had already darted out of the room and was running down the corridor to whip open Binky's neighbour's door.

'Aha!' cried Friday. Then she realised it was just Epstein lying on the floor, having apparently fallen off a chair. 'Oh, it's you.'

Epstein was rubbing his shin and wincing. His desk chair was lying on its side. Friday glanced about the room. She noticed there was an air vent in the shared wall between Epstein's room and Binky's.

'Were you listening in to our conversation next door?' asked Friday.

'No,' said Epstein.

'Then why were you standing on a chair?' asked Friday.

'I was changing a lightbulb,' said Epstein.

Friday looked at the illuminated lightbulb. 'Your lightbulb doesn't need changing,' she observed.

'I'd just finished changing it,' said Epstein.

Friday glanced in the rubbish bin. It was empty. 'Then where is the old bulb?'

Epstein didn't say anything. He just pouted.

'You're a terrible liar,' said Friday.

'All Binky does is exercise and snore loudly,' said Epstein. 'Of course I was going to be curious when he suddenly has a whole group of people in his room, having some sort of animated conversation.'

'Did you hear anyone enter Binky's room in the last half hour?' asked Friday.

'No,' said Epstein, shaking his head.

'Really?' said Friday. 'My friend Melanie can tell if a person is lying.'

Friday turned to Melanie.

'He's not,' said Melanie. 'And it's easy to tell when Epstein's lying because his face goes red. Although his face is already red from hurting himself in the fall. But even so, I know he's not lying.'

'So someone silently snuck into Binky's room and stuck the "The Red Princess" to the back of his picture,' said Friday.

'You found "The Red Princess"?' said Epstein.

'Yes,' said Friday. 'I suppose we had better return it to the Headmaster and Mr Brecht.'

Mr Brecht stared long and hard at the painting for about five seconds before surprising everyone by bursting into laughter. Friday, Melanie, Binky, Epstein and Ian had all gathered in the Headmaster's office. They had expected yelling and recriminations, possibly tears. They hadn't expected the great artist to find it funny.

'Aren't you upset that your painting has been vandalised?' asked Friday.

'I don't know,' said Mr Brecht, taking a closer look. 'Whoever did it has nice brushstrokes. Who's to say it's not an improvement?'

'But it's not your original artistic vision anymore,' said Ian.

'Most of that stuff is all twaddle,' said Mr Brecht. 'A good conservator will be able to remove the black hair easily enough. It's a prank. An elegantly executed prank. I'm not going to get my knickers in a twist over that.'

'Thank you, Mr Brecht,' said the Headmaster. 'On behalf of the school, we're grateful that you can be so understanding. It appears that we are not able to display the painting with the security it requires. If you would like to arrange for it to be stored somewhere safely – a bank vault, perhaps . . .'

'Hang it in the reception area, for all I care,' said Mr Brecht. 'Miss Priddock will keep an eye on it. Or, rather, anybody who comes in will have an eye on her and not notice the painting.'

'Aren't you worried that there might be another attack on the picture?' asked Friday.

'I'm sure whoever the prankster is has enjoyed their little joke and is ready to move on with their life,' said Mr Brecht. 'Now that's all resolved, if you don't mind, I need to get back to my classroom.'

'You have a class waiting?' asked the Headmaster.

'No, a lovely Camembert cheese,' said Mr Brecht as he headed out the door. 'I've been looking forward to having it for afternoon tea.'

'He seems awfully relaxed about the whole thing,' said Melanie. 'I'm all for being relaxed, but he seems to be taking relaxation to a new level.'

'Probably been breathing in too many paint fumes,' said Epstein.

'I suspect Mr Brecht knows something we don't,' said Friday.

'Everyone knows something I don't,' said Melanie.

Chapter 7

The Mystery of the Missing Time

Friday headed towards her history classroom. She knew she was going to be early, but that suited her just fine. It would give her a chance to read her book. Now that the painting had been recovered, Friday could relax and really enjoy *An Analysis of Gut Bacteria*. She never realised you could know so much about a person from the microorganisms living in their intestines.

Melanie wasn't with Friday because she had been given a detention by the PE teacher for refusing to do a star jump. Their previous PE teacher had long ago given up trying to get Melanie to do anything. But the new teacher, Mr Fontana, was young and enthusiastic and hadn't realised the enormous strength of will Melanie was capable of when it came to refusing to do any form of exercise.

Melanie claimed she was a conscientious objector. The teacher declared that Melanie would not be allowed to go to lunch until she had completed just one repetition of the exercise. So Friday had done the only thing she could for her friend. She'd gone to the dining hall, picked up an extra serving of frittata, wrapped it in foil and put it on Melanie's desk so she could eat it later. She had one hundred per cent confidence in her friend that the star jump would not be performed.

It was nice entering the history classroom all by herself. It was a large room with portraits of British monarchs across the back wall, big windows letting in lots of natural light, and ceiling fans creating a pleasant breeze. Friday picked the stool at the back, furthest away from the teacher's desk, sat down and got out her book.

As she was finding her page, she noticed movement out of the corner of her eye.

That was the last thing she would remember.

Everything was black. Except for the stars swirling around on the inside of her eyelids.

Friday's head throbbed terribly. It was like the pulse of her blood was squeezing her brain.

'Friday? Friday!'

Friday could hear the voices calling to her, but she didn't want to reply or even open her eyes in case it encouraged them. She just wanted them to shut up and go away so she could drift back into unconsciousness and no longer feel this dreadful headache.

'Friday?'

Friday recognised that voice. It was Melanie. She opened her eyes. She immediately regretted the decision. The blindingly bright light made the drum in her head pound louder.

'Did you do the star jump?' she asked weakly.

'Goodness, no,' said Melanie. 'I might seem laid-back, but I do have principles.'

Friday closed her eyes, deciding that going back to sleep would be the best thing for this terrible pain in her head.

'Friday?' said Melanie again.

'What?' moaned Friday.

'What happened?' asked the Headmaster.

'What?' said Friday. She couldn't understand what was going on and the effort to think was making her head hurt more. 'Why are you here? Doesn't Miss Bertram teach me history?'

'I'm over here, dear,' said Miss Bertram.

'You are lying on the floor of the history classroom,' said Melanie.

'Miss Bertram called me when you were found unconscious,' said the Headmaster.

Friday thought about this for a moment. It didn't make any sense. She opened her eyes, just a crack this time. There was a lot of people crowded round her, but it certainly looked like the history classroom and there was the distinctive smell of modelling glue used in the dioramas that decorated the room. She wished she hadn't noticed the smell. Now she felt like throwing up.

'Maybe you should sit up,' suggested Melanie.

Friday felt several pairs of hands grab her by the arms and gently help her up into the sitting position.

'Do you know you've got a big lump on your forehead?' asked Melanie.

Friday reached up and touched her forehead. It felt like someone had glued half an egg to the middle. It really hurt.

'Did you get in a fight with someone?' asked the Headmaster.

'I wouldn't be surprised,' said Mirabella Peterson. 'She's so annoying.'

'I don't know,' said Friday.

'What's the last thing you remember?' asked Melanie.

'I was early, so I got out my book to read,' said Friday. 'I'm reading about the anatomy of gut bacteria.'

'That's how she hurt her head then,' said Mirabella. 'The book is so boring she slipped into a coma and hit her head on the table.'

'Where is my book?' asked Friday, starting to worry.

'You've got a head injury,' said Melanie. 'I don't think that's important right now.'

'Of course it is,' said Friday. 'The librarian hates me enough. I can't lose the book.'

Friday started looking about. It was hard to see through the forest of legs.

'Here it is,' called Patel. He hurried over to the far side of the room and picked up the paperback book, then brought it to Friday.

'That's a relief,' said Friday. 'I was just getting to a good bit about gluten intolerance.' She took the book and noticed there was a large dent in the middle of it. 'Someone's attacked my book!' she exclaimed.

'Someone bashes you on the head and it's the dent in your book that you find shocking?' said Melanie.

'It looks like someone has hit it with a knife or a ruler,' said Friday, peering at the pages. 'The dent has gone right through the cover and affected half the pages.'

'The police are on their way,' said the Headmaster.

'Why?' asked Friday.

The Headmaster sighed. Friday was irritating when she was thinking clearly, but apparently she was even more irritating when she couldn't think at all. 'Because you've been attacked,' he said, slowly and clearly.

'Oh,' said Friday. She was finding it hard to concentrate on what people were saying. Something wasn't right. She tried to focus on the portrait of Henry VIII on the wall. It was off somehow.

'Barnes!' snapped the Headmaster. 'Are you listening to me?'

'Why is Henry the Eighth wearing a Swatch wrist watch?' asked Friday, as everyone turned to look at the polka-dot watch that had been painted onto his wrist in a careful imitation of the sixteenth-century painting style. Then Friday lost consciousness again.

When Friday woke up, Sergeant Crowley was standing over her.

'So was it the boyfriend?' asked Sergeant Crowley. 'What's his name again?'

'Ian Wainscott,' said Melanie.

'He's not my boyfriend,' said Friday weakly.

'She's concussed. She doesn't know what she's saying.' said Melanie.

'Whatever their relationship, I'll want to ask him a few questions,' said Sergeant Crowley.

'We don't have a relationship,' protested Friday. She tried to summon the energy to stand up, but all she did was raise her hand a little bit off the floor. 'What are you even doing here? Surely I haven't been unconscious that long. It takes half an hour for you to drive here from the police station.'

'I was already on school grounds,' said Sergeant Crowley.

'Were you arresting Mr Fontana?' asked Melanie.

'No, why should I arrest him?' asked Sergeant Crowley.

'Oh, no reason,' said Melanie. 'But he did try to force me to do a star jump this morning, so I assume he's capable of anything.'

'Let's just deal with the matter of the assault on Miss Barnes first,' said the sergeant, taking out his notebook and pen. 'Does she have any other enemies?'

'Oh, lots and lots,' said Melanie. 'All her teachers, all the students she's had suspended or punished and then all the people she just irritates.'

'It could have been anybody,' said Mirabella. 'I'd be tempted to do it myself.'

'Really?' said the Sergeant Crowley. 'And what's your name?'

'Me?!' exclaimed Mirabella. 'Trea Dawson.'

Trea was Mirabella's cheerleading rival. Everyone sniggered.

'Stop,' said Friday feebly. 'I was not attacked.'

'Then how do you explain the blunt force trauma injury to your head?' asked the Sergeant Crowley. 'I've had a look at that lump. You've clearly been struck very hard by a thin weapon. Like a stick or a ruler.'

'No, no,' said Friday groggily. 'I think . . . I think, I remember . . . it was a rat.'

'So it was Ian?!' said Melanie.

'No, a literal rat,' said Friday. 'One that squeaks and scurries around.'

'I don't think a rat would have the strength to hit you with a stick,' said Melanie.

'It can't have been a person,' said Friday. 'Why would they have put my book all the way over there?'

'Perhaps they have a lot of anger towards boring books?' said Melanie.

'And why was the book struck as well?' asked Friday.

'Maybe you held up the book defensively and they struck it first?' said Sergeant Crowley.

'No, Friday wouldn't do that,' said Melanie. 'She'd be more likely to stick her head in front to protect the book.'

'I'll show you what happened,' said Friday as she slowly got to her feet. Several classmates helped her over to the stool, where she sat down again. 'I was sitting here, reading, when I saw something move out of the corner of my eye.'

'Your attacker?' asked the Sergeant Crowley.

'In a way, yes,' said Friday. 'I saw a rat. Now, you have to understand I am not normally a hysterical female. I pride myself on being rational, and not embracing derogatory gender stereotypes. But I had just been reading all about bacteria and disease and nothing is more famous for spreading bacteria and disease than a rat. It caught me unawares, and I was alarmed. So I did what you always see people do on television and in movies. I stood up on my chair.'

'So?' said Sergeant Crowley.

'See for yourself,' said Friday, pointing at the spinning ceiling fan. 'We don't notice ceiling fans because they are so ubiquitous. It's odd, really, because the blades are spinning in excess of forty kilometres per hour at such a short distance from our heads.'

'You stuck your head in a ceiling fan?' asked Melanie.

'Just because I'm highly intelligent, doesn't mean I can't be stupid,' said Friday.

'I don't know,' said Sergeant Crowley. 'I still think it's more plausible that someone hit you over the head.'

'I can prove it was the fan,' said Friday.

'She's going to stick her head in it again!' said Mirabella excitedly.

Friday picked up her *An Analysis of Gut Bacteria*. It was damaged already, so she had nothing left to lose. And then, with a surprisingly accurate toss that would have made the PE teacher proud, she threw the book up into the blades of the moving fan. The fan instantly smacked into the book and flung it across the room like a cricket ball, narrowly missing Patel's head.

'You see, the fan hit me,' said Friday. 'I flung up my arms, throwing the book into the fan after me. It shot across the room and I fell on the floor, hitting my head for a second time, and passing out.'

'Well, this is quite something,' said Sergeant Crowley, putting his notebook and pen back in his pocket. 'First, the opium plant in the rose bed turns out to be a plastic Remembrance Day poppy, and now the attacker in the classroom turns out to be a ceiling fan. That's two wild goose chases in one day.'

'Shouldn't it be geese chases then?' asked Melanie.

'I could still arrest you for being a public nuisance,' said the sergeant, glowering at Melanie.

'Oh, you'd never do that,' said Melanie. 'Just think of all the lawyers my father would send to yell at you. If you think I'm a nuisance, they're much worse.'

The school bell rang.

'Oh good, it's the end of history class,' said Melanie.

'I didn't get time to teach you anything,' complained Miss Bertram.

'Don't worry, Miss Bertram,' said Melanie. 'We probably wouldn't have listened anyway.'

Chapter 8

Art Class

Friday went with Melanie to see the nurse during morning break. The nurse gave her an icepack and a plastic bucket to carry with her in case she was sick, then declared that Friday would be all right to continue with classes so long as they didn't involve body-contact sports.

'We've got art next,' Melanie told her. 'Friday will be fine. She never does much in art anyway, except look confused.'

'Walk there slowly,' advised the nurse. 'And don't let her breathe in too many paint fumes.'

'That's two head injuries now,' Melanie said to Friday. 'First the picnic table, and now the fan. You'd better watch out, these things happen in threes.'

'I think that's only for celebrity deaths, not head injuries,' said Friday. 'Come on, let's get to class.'

Art had never been Friday's favourite subject. She struggled with the concept of emotionally expressing herself at the best of times. But emotionally expressing yourself through two-dimensional pictorial representations was a concept that was beyond her.

Even when it came to realism, she struggled. She found it hard to be motivated to draw a bowl of fruit when a photograph would provide a much more accurate representation. Friday still had the same feeling she had as a preschooler when she was asked to finger paint. She felt like she was entirely missing the point of the exercise.

Mr Brecht was five minutes late for his first class. This surprised Friday. Usually the lateness of teachers could be gauged by how much damage thirty students could do with the contents of their classroom. As such, a history teacher rarely turned up in the first ten minutes because their classroom just contained chairs and tables. Whereas chemistry, woodwork and art teachers were always punctual because you could do a lot of damage with a storage room full of chemicals, lumber or paint. (In fact, if you combined all three you could even make a doomsday device.)

Melanie was starting to drift off to sleep by the time Mr Brecht bounded in through the front door carrying a large green duffel bag.

'Year 7?' he asked.

'Yes, sir,' said Mirabella Peterson.

Friday was impressed how much simpering she managed to inject into those two short words.

'Good,' said Mr Brecht, dumping his big bag on the floor. 'I've got eight weeks to teach you how to be artists. What have you been working on so far this year?'

'Plein-air impressionist paintings of the school grounds,' said Peregrine.

'Blah, how boring,' said Mr Brecht, with disgust. He picked up the copy of the year 7 syllabus that had been laid out for him on the desk, glanced at it, then threw it in the wastepaper bin. 'I'm sure we can come up with something more interesting than that. Let's do some finger painting.'

'You can't be serious,' said Friday.

Melanie kicked her under the table. 'It is a social convention to not be outwardly rude to a person the first time you meet them.'

'But you're supposed to be the greatest artist in the country,' continued Friday, 'and finger painting is something we already covered in preschool.'

'And preschool was probably the last time you did a good painting,' said Mr Brecht, sitting down and putting his feet up on the desk. Friday noted that his shoes needed resoling. 'Which is why we are going right back to square one to build you into proper artists from the ground up.'

BANG, BANG, BANG.

They all heard knocking.

'What was that?' asked Mr Brecht.

The door to the classroom was wide open and no one was there. The knocking sound came again.

BANG, BANG, BANG.

It was coming from the storage room. Mr Brecht swung his feet down, prowled over to the door and pressed his ear against it. 'Is anybody in there?'

'Please let me out!' pleaded a voice from inside.

'Where's the key?' Mr Brecht asked the class.

'Didn't they give you keys to the classroom when they gave you the job?' asked Melanie.

'I suppose so,' said Mr Brecht. 'But I don't know where I left them.'

'Normally Friday would pick the lock for you,' said Melanie. 'But I don't know if she's up to it, since the blow to her head.'

'I'll try,' said Friday, standing up from her stool. She walked over to the closet door and bent down to have a look. She stared at it for several long moments before she slowly overbalanced and landed on her face. 'Sorry, I can't remember how to do it,' she said confusedly from the floor.

'Please let me out,' pleaded the voice from the closet. 'I've been in here for hours. I'm starving.'

'Stand back,' ordered Mr Brecht, yelling through the timber. 'Get away from the door!'

There was the muffled sound of the boy shuffling out of the way. Mr Brecht took a step back, lifted his leg and powerfully slammed the ball of his foot into the door just below the lock. The door ripped out of the frame and flew back, hitting something just behind it.

'Ow,' said the voice.

Mr Brecht strode into the closet, and looked behind the door. He reached down and pulled up Travis, a short, curly haired year 8 boy. Blood was streaming from his nose.

'I told you to get away from the door,' said Mr Brecht.

'I thought standing behind it would be the safest spot,' said Travis.

'Why were you in the closet in the first place?' asked Mr Brecht.

'I was locked in there by a bully,' said Travis.

'Who?' asked Mr Brecht.

'Ian Wainscott,' said Travis.

'What?!' said Ian. 'I'm standing right here.'

Travis looked alarmed to see Ian. He clearly hadn't known that Ian was in the room.

'I might have been wrong,' said Travis. 'I know it was a big boy. I assumed it was Ian, because it's just the nasty sort of prank he's always pulling.'

This clearly made Ian proud because he smiled smugly at the compliment.

Mr Brecht went back into the closet and looked about. He came back, looking cross. 'You ate my snacks!' he exclaimed. 'I had a wheel of brie cheese and a whole packet of water crackers in there and now they're gone! Or, rather, they're mostly gone because you left a pile of crumbs.'

'I was starving,' protested Travis. 'I've been in there since first thing this morning. I missed out on pancakes for breakfast.'

'Ooh, they were good,' said Melanie. 'Mrs Marigold's surprise pancakes are my favourite! This crime is far more serious than I first imagined. It's one thing to lock an annoying boy in a closet – we've all wanted to do that – but to lock him in on one of the rare mornings when Mrs Marigold is cooking pancakes? That's just plain cruel.'

'He's lying,' said Friday.

Everyone turned to look at her. They had forgotten about Friday in all the excitement. Friday was sitting on the floor. She still seemed confused and was rubbing her head.

'Friday, perhaps you'd better lie down,' said Melanie. 'You look like my dog Bertie after Daddy accidentally hit him with his electric golf cart.'

'No, let her speak,' said Ian. 'I want her to clear my name.'

'Travis can't have been waylaid on the way to breakfast,' said Friday, 'because the pancakes were a surprise. No one knew about them until we arrived at the dining hall.'

'I guessed,' said Travis.

'No, we always have muesli on Wednesdays,' said Friday. 'If you had guessed, you would have guessed that.'

'Then someone must have told me as I was walking to the dining hall,' said Travis.

'Then how did you come to be locked in the closet?' said Friday 'Even Mr Brecht doesn't have a key.'

'I don't know,' said Travis. 'Perhaps the bully had a copy.'

'Turn out your pockets,' said Friday.

Travis emptied out his pockets. They were empty. 'See!' he declared. 'It's not fair, sir. I've suffered a trauma and she's blaming me, the victim.'

'Well, you are annoying,' said Melanie. 'It would be anyone's natural instinct.'

Friday gingerly got to her feet and walked over to the closet. She looked inside. There were long, deep shelves stacked with heavy paint bottles, buckets of acrylic primer, reams of paper and glue by the gallon.

On the floor in front of the art reference books was a scattered pile of biscuit crumbs.

'And here we have the motive,' said Friday, pointing towards the reference books.

'Books?' said Mr Brecht. 'How are they a motive?'

'This is a school,' said Friday. 'Travis is a hormonal teenager. And those books would have the only pictures in the school featuring naked ladies.'

'It's not true!' protested Travis.

Friday picked up a book on European portraiture that was lying on the ground. 'If you pick up a book and open it quickly so that each side of the cover is lying on the horizontal palm of your hand,' said Friday, 'the book will naturally fall open to where it was read last. It's got to do with the stretching and bending of the paper and cardboard in the spine. Like this . . .' Friday opened the book so that the covers were against her palms and the pages fanned out in an arch. They slowly flicked to their final resting place. 'Ah, just as I suspected: the Renaissance. Rembrandt and Rubens. Really, I have to congratulate Travis on going against the contemporary objectification of women and showing interest in classical beauty values.'

'Maybe I just like art,' said Travis, snatching the book away from Friday.

'I'm sure you do,' said Friday. 'But this art was specifically created because men like looking at naked ladies. Really you were enjoying art appreciation in its truest sense.'

'Then where's the key?' asked Mr Brecht in frustration. 'Clearly, I have to be able to lock this closet if I'm going to enjoy my own cheese.'

Friday looked about. 'We have to think like Travis. He's in here eating cheese, looking at pictures, when he hears the other students arrive. He realises it's too late to sneak out, so he decides to pretend he's been locked in. So he has to hide the key. The problem for us is there are so many possibilities. He could drop it into a bottle of glue or paint and the only way we'd find it is by emptying all the paint out in the closet.'

'We can't do that. There are thousands of dollars' worth of paint in here,' said Mr Brecht.

Friday turned to Travis. 'Show me your fingernails.'

Travis dug his hands in his pocket. 'No, you can't search me without a search warrant.'

'Really?' said Friday. 'That means you know your fingernails would give you away.' She looked across at the shelf directly opposite the reference books. There sat one big block of clay, wrapped in plastic. She peeled back the wrapping from the top. The clay was perfectly smooth.

'The surface is undisturbed,' said Mr Brecht.

'It's clay,' said Friday. 'It would be easy enough to smooth down.' She reached into her pocket and took out her own dorm room key, then started to gouge a long line through the top of the clay.

'What are you doing?' demanded Mr Brecht. 'I need to use that clay for this afternoon's year 8 class.'

'It's in here somewhere,' said Friday. 'Aha!' Her key had struck something. Friday dug her finger in and gouged out another key. 'The key to the art closet.'

'But anyone could have put that there,' protested Travis, pointing at the key. Ian reached over and grabbed him by the wrist. 'Let's have a look at your fingers,' he said.

Travis's fingers were covered in dried clay.

'Young man,' said Mr Brecht quietly, which only made what he said more menacing, 'if you want to look at the art reference books, you can do so at any time. But a more serious crime has been committed here. You owe me a cheese. I expect that cheese to be replaced by the end of the week, and not with some locally made rubbish. A proper brie imported from France using dangerously unhealthy unpasteurised milk. Do I make myself clear?'

'Yes, sir,' said Travis.

'Now, come on, let's get to work,' snapped Mr Brecht.

Chapter 9

The First Lesson

'I've seen what your old art teacher taught you,' said Mr Brecht, 'and it's all a load of rubbish.'

'All of it?' asked Melanie.

'Pointless busy work,' declared Mr Brecht, 'getting you to use cheap acrylic paint and bog-standard cartridge paper. That's never going to inspire you to be great artists.'

'Da Vinci did lots of drawing on paper,' said Friday.

'And what's his legacy?' asked Mr Brecht. 'Seven oil paintings. One of which the paint is peeling off because he used flawed, experimental techniques. What's the point of painting a mural of the Last Supper if you're going to use paint that peels off? He was painting a church wall, not a seven-year-old girl's fingernails.'

'So what are we going to do?' asked Melanie.

'I'm going to teach you how to do proper oil painting on proper canvas, like real artists,' announced Mr Brecht. He opened up his duffel bag and took out several plain white canvases. 'Here, hand them around.'

'They're rather big,' noted Melanie. Each canvas was at least one square metre.

'That's the whole point,' said Mr Brecht. 'I want you to have big ideas, to express all your feelings. If you paint on a small piece of paper, you can only have small ideas and small feelings. Let your emotions out.'

The class started distributing the frames. Friday got hers. She was surprised how impressive it felt to hold. It was a proper timber frame with canvas coated in thick white paint.

'Luckily for you, your headmaster is an idiot,' said Mr Brecht. 'He's given me an enormous budget. So I've bought you the best supplies. Cedar frames, French cloth, and I primed the canvases myself. You'll never make a masterpiece on paper. It's like drawing on a children's menu at a pizza restaurant.'

'I like this teacher,' Melanie said to Friday. 'He sounds like fun . . . in a deranged, egomaniacal sort of way.'

'At the end of my eight weeks here trying to drum talent into you,' continued Mr Brecht, 'the Head-master wants to hold an art show to display your work, which will be auctioned off to the highest bidder.'

'Who would want to buy paintings by a bunch of high-school students?' asked Friday.

'Their super rich parents,' said Mr Brecht. 'So I'm sure we'll raise quite a bit of money.'

'For charity?' asked Friday.

'If you call a private school's indoor swimming pool fund a charity, then yes,' said Mr Brecht.

'But the school doesn't have a swimming pool,' said Friday.

'That's what the fund is going to rectify,' said Mr Brecht. 'Capitalism is wonderful, isn't it?'

Friday was still suffering the effects of her blow to her head. Apart from the splitting headache, her thoughts were very fuzzy indeed. She was finding it hard to concentrate long enough to remember what a sentence was about by the time anyone had finished saying it. But she had got the gist that she was meant to be painting.

'What do you want us to paint?' Friday asked.

'Whatever you want,' said Mr Brecht.

'Can you narrow it down?' asked Friday.

'Something that makes you passionate,' said Mr Brecht.

'Friday doesn't do passion,' said Ian.

'I thought she was your girlfriend,' said Peregrine.

'They're having a long, drawn-out fight,' said Melanie, 'because Friday made Ian uncomfortably aware of how little his father cares for him.'

'I don't know why he doesn't,' said Friday. 'Ian is very nice –'

'Did you hear that?!' said Melanie. 'The concussion is making her speak the truth!'

'– when he isn't being a total pompous bore,' continued Friday. 'Which is only about three per cent of the time.'

'And she reverts to character,' said Ian.

'When I say passionate,' said Mr Brecht, 'I don't mean "love".'

'We're not talking about love, either,' said Ian.

'I was,' said Melanie.

'It can be something that makes you passionately angry,' said Mr Brecht. 'Or deeply sad. Or insanely jealous.'

'I can think of several things,' said Ian, glaring at Friday.

'Good,' said Mr Brecht. 'Now, all of you, shut up and get painting. I don't want to hear a word out of you until your canvas is covered. Anyone who speaks will have to buy me another cheese.' Mr Brecht leaned back in his chair and closed his eyes. The class set to work.

Friday pondered her emotions. She had a lot of them. Her looming antagonism with Ian had worn her down. She did feel angry, and resentful, and even just plain irritated. But that was all on the surface. When she dug deep into the strata of her emotions (something she had never done before but now found she was able to, thanks to the clarity of thinking her head injury had allowed her) she realised that, underneath it all, she felt very sad.

Ian was just the tip of the iceberg protruding above the surface of her despair. Beneath, she had a lot of sadness with her family, but also with herself and her own inadequacies – the things that prevented her from having more than one friend. From being able to hold a socially acceptable conversation. To fit in, blend in and melt away in comfortable familiarity. Friday had never realised how sad she felt about all these things; she thought she was proud to not need them. But humans are pack animals. They naturally seek out community and belonging.

'Excellent!'

Friday turned around when she realised that the voice was from outside her head, not her inner monologue.

'Excuse me,' said Friday.

'Your painting is beautiful,' said Mr Brecht. 'I've never seen a child of your age express emotion so poignantly on canvas.'

'I have?' said Friday. She hadn't even thought about what she was painting. 'I just painted what I was feeling. Like you said.'

Friday looked back at her canvas. It was a savage tapestry of vivid blue and brown strokes, skewered in the centre by two haunting, dead black eyes. Friday realised she had painted a self-portrait.

'Wow,' said Melanie.

'Have you ever considered seeing a psychiatrist?' asked Mirabella, looking genuinely scared.

Ian came over and studied Friday's work. 'I think Friday should be taken to the nurse,' said Ian. 'The knock to her head is more serious than we thought. If it's made her capable of feeling human emotion, she may have suffered brain damage.'

Chapter 10

Golf

The next day, Friday had a terrible headache. But her brain was working normally, at least normally for her. She sat in the corner of the dining hall, tentatively picking at her serving of blancmange. Friday was trying to move as little as possible, because every movement or sudden loud noise would make her flinch. And every time she flinched she felt like someone had hit her in the head with an axe.

Luckily, Melanie was the perfect companion to have in times such as these. Melanie had a gift for being silent, especially when she was asleep.

Friday was slowly making her way through the food and was just starting to feel slightly better, when there was a loud bang, and the crashing of crockery.

Friday's first instinct was to roll up in the foetal position, clamp her hands over her ears and wait for it all to be over. But that didn't seem to be happening. The noise continued and, if anything, grew louder. Now there were shouts of abuse.

'You stinking cheat!'

'How dare you! I did no such thing!'

'Next you'll be saying fairies moved the ball!'

'I did not cheat!'

Friday slowly turned to see Tom Malik and Stephan Bauer wrestling. They were rolling back and forth along one of the long table tops, knocking off cutlery and laden plates as they grappled. As every plate or fork hit the ground, it might as well have been hitting Friday directly in the head, it hurt so much.

'What's going on?' asked Friday.

'I don't know,' said Melanie. 'It sounds like it's

some sort of disagreement, but you can never tell with boys. When they act like this, sometimes I think they just want a hug.'

Friday got up and slowly walked over to the two wrestling boys. They were on the ground now, banging benches and tables, which made awful scraping noises as the furniture was bumped back and forth across the linoleum floor.

'Stop it,' said Friday.

The boys ignored her and kept wrestling. Tom was trying to rub a handful of mashed potato in Stephan's hair, and Stephan was trying to bang Tom's head on a table leg.

Friday sighed. There was a large jug of water on the table. She picked it up and poured it over the boys' heads.

'Hey! What did you do that for?' demanded Tom.

'Now we're all wet,' protested Stephan.

'You two are ruining lunch for everybody with your loudness and violence,' said Friday. 'If you're going to try to hurt each other, go and do it outside.'

'You'd like that, wouldn't you?' accused Stephan, turning on Tom. 'If we went outside, he'd probably use the opportunity to attack me from behind.'

'You're paranoid,' accused Tom. 'And deranged.'

Friday rubbed her forehead. The pain was definitely getting worse.

'If you want some peace and quiet again,' said Melanie, 'it might be quickest just to solve their problem for them.'

'I can't cure them of being idiots,' grumbled Friday.

'No,' agreed Melanie, 'but they are arguing about something, and perhaps it's something you could settle with your detective skills.'

'All right, all right,' said Friday. 'Boys, I will get to the bottom of whatever it is you're fighting about and work out who really is at fault. On one condition.'

'You want us to pay you?' asked Tom.

'No, my condition is that you will both shut up,' said Friday. 'You will speak only when spoken to and then only in a very soft voice, as if I were a timid mouse and you were frightened I would run away.'

Melanie made a scoffing noise. 'Yeah right, as if you would run anywhere.'

'Okay,' continued Friday, 'using your quietest indoors voices, tell me what happened. From the beginning.'

'It was the inter-house golf championship yester-day,' said Tom.

'I'll just nod and pretend I know what that is,' said Friday. 'Continue.'

'We were the top contenders to win,' explained Stephan. 'We're the number two and three players in the team.'

'Who's number one?' asked Melanie.

'Ian Wainscott,' said Tom.

Friday winced.

'He always wins,' added Stephan. 'But he wasn't competing yesterday.'

'How come?' asked Melanie. She turned to Friday. 'You don't mind if I ask these questions for you, do you? It's obviously a painful subject for you to discuss.'

Friday had closed her eyes and waved her hand for Melanie to continue the line of questioning.

'So why wasn't Ian playing?' asked Melanie.

'He had too many detentions,' said Tom. 'If you get three or more detentions in a week, you can't play comp sport.'

'It's a rule to encourage gentleman-like behaviour off the field,' explained Stephan.

'Really?' said Melanie. 'Sport has such strange concepts of ethics.'

'So, for the first time this year, Tom and I had a chance of winning,' continued Stephan. 'And he decided to cheat.'

'I did not!' protested Tom. He looked like he was about to grab Stephan again, so Friday held up her hand to get their attention.

'Take me to the scene of the crime,' she said. 'And no more bickering.'

'Okay,' said Tom, 'but it's a bit of a walk. It happened on the seventeenth hole.'

'Urgh,' Friday shuddered. Her headache had made any form of bright light painful to endure, and it was a sunny day outside. 'All right, if you find me a pair of sunglasses I'll go out to the golf course with you to have a look.'

Ten minutes later, Friday, Melanie, Tom and Stephan were striding out towards the seventeenth hole of the golf course. It was a long, hilly walk, which wound around trees, bushes, water features and strange sculptures depicting heroes from Greek mythology.

'Is it normal for golf courses to be randomly decorated with statues?' asked Friday.

'Not really,' said Stephan. 'It can affect the game when your ball bounces off one. I hit a ball off Achilles once and it bounced into a sand trap.'

'Some elderly benefactor donated them to the school,' explained Tom. 'I think they just put them around the golf course so they'd be out of the way.'

By the time they crossed the sixteenth fairway, they had lost sight of the school behind them. If it weren't for the unnaturally green grass beneath their feet it would be as if they were in a forest. It was so tranquil to be surrounded by nature.

'The seventeenth tee is just up and around those bushes,' said Stephan.

They climbed around the bend and were surprised to discover someone sitting on a rock. It was Epstein. He was furiously scribbling in a notebook.

'What are you doing here?' asked Friday.

Epstein looked up and slammed the notebook

shut. He looked guilty, as if he'd been caught out. 'Nothing.'

'That's a lie,' said Melanie.

'I can see that,' said Friday. 'Clearly he's writing in a notebook. What I meant was, why is he writing in a notebook out here?'

'That's none of your business,' said Epstein.

Friday sighed. 'Fine, have your secrets. I'll just assume you're meeting someone here.'

'There could be another reason,' said Melanie. 'Perhaps he doesn't want anyone to find out what he's writing.'

'Notes for a criminal plot?' asked Friday.

'I was thinking love poetry,' said Melanie. 'But it could be a criminal plot to impress his one true love.'

'You've been reading romance novels again, haven't you?' said Friday.

'Yes,' agreed Melanie.

'Good,' said Friday. 'It's important to read.'

Epstein stood up. 'If I can't have some peace and quiet, I'm going back.' He stalked off, back towards the school.

'But what about your rendezvous?' Melanie called after him. 'If we come across any nice girls out here, we'll know they're clues.'

With Epstein gone, they all stepped up onto the seventeenth tee and looked out down the fairway.

'What a pretty view,' remarked Melanie.

Friday had not considered it in that light. She was too busy focusing on how, even with the sunglasses, the sunlight was burning holes in her retinas, or how the frogs croaking in the nearby creak were unnaturally loud. But now that she looked out at the golf course she realised Melanie was right. It was very pretty.

From the tee the fairway swept down into a gully, then up again, bending along the creek towards the elevated green. Oak trees lined either side and a picturesque, although undoubtedly troublesome to a golfer, duck pond sat bathed in sunlight off to the right.

'So this is the starting point?' asked Friday. She knew nothing about golf, except that it involved small white balls and men wearing silly trousers.

'Yes, this is the tee,' said Tom. 'It's where you hit off from.'

'I hit a straight drive right up the middle of the fairway,' said Stephan. 'It flew 150 metres before the first bounce and then rolled another twenty metres up the hill. It was a beautiful shot.'

'And you?' asked Friday, turning to Tom.

Tom frowned. 'I shanked it.'

'What does that mean?' Friday turned to Melanie.

'Don't ask me,' said Melanie.

'He sliced it,' said Stephan, then sensing Friday's withering glare he explained further. 'He hit the ball wrong, so that instead of going straight it arced away into the trees.'

'It hit the trunk of an oak and bounced into the rough,' continued Tom. 'It could only have ended up forty metres from the tee.'

'Oh,' said Melanie. 'And that's bad because you were trying to hit the ball all the way up there to that flaggy thing?' She pointed at the flag four hundred metres away on the distant green.

'That's right,' said Tom.

'So how are you saying he cheated?' asked Friday. 'Are you accusing him of setting up a rubber oak tree, or tampering with your ball, or distracting you during your swing?'

'I don't know how he did it!' exclaimed Stephan. 'But he did. We spent ten minutes searching for his ball in the trees but we couldn't find it anywhere.'

'So the ball was lost,' said Friday.

'No,' said Stephan. 'We found the ball, all right. When we got up to the green it was sitting slap bang in the middle – just a few centimetres from the hole.'

'I got lucky,' said Tom with a shrug. 'I didn't do anything.'

'There is no way luck or anything other than an extreme, miniaturised tornado could have made your ball travel all the way up there,' said Stephan.

'It does seem to defy the laws of physics,' said Friday as she winced into the distance, gauging the distance to the hole. 'It must be four hundred metres. Can you hit a ball four hundred metres?'

'Not usually,' admitted Tom.

'He cheated because he knows I'm naturally more talented,' said Stephan.

'No way!' exclaimed Tom. 'You choke when you putt.'

'Only because you're always humming when I'm trying to hit the ball!' yelled Stephan. The two boys grabbed each other's collars and looked ready to resume fighting again.

'Excuse me, would you mind if I play through?'

Friday turned to see Ian standing right behind her. He had a golf bag on his shoulder and a driver in his hand, all ready to tee off.

'What are you doing here?' asked Friday.

'Playing golf,' said Ian. 'It is why most people come out here to the golf course.'

'I thought you were banned for getting too many detentions,' said Friday.

'I was excluded from the weekly tournament,' said Ian. 'I'm still allowed to practise. Speaking of which, do you mind? If you four are going to stand around fighting, I'd like to play through.'

Friday looked at the ball in Ian's hand. 'Please do,' she said. 'I need to perform an experiment, and if you hit a ball out there onto the fairway it will save me from having to learn golf and hit one out there myself.'

Ian scoffed. 'You'd have to have a total body and brain transplant to play. This is a sport. It requires balance and coordination.'

'Yes, but it isn't a very sporty sport,' said Melanie.

'You don't have to slam into anyone, or run, or get sweaty, or out of breath. So, if you think about it, Friday is more likely to be good at this than any other physical exercise.'

'Really?' said Ian. 'By all means. Have a go.' He held out the driver to Friday.

'No,' said Friday. 'There is nothing to be gained for this investigation by me humiliating myself. But seeing you hit the ball out there would be a very beneficial experiment, so please go ahead.'

Ian turned, pressed a tee into the ground and balanced his ball on top. He looked up at the fairway, planning his shot, then took his stance.

Tom grabbed Friday by the elbow and pulled her back several paces.

'What are you doing?' asked Friday.

'If you stand there, you'll get hit in the head by his backswing,' said Tom. 'And if you're going to clear me of cheating, I don't want you getting another head injury.'

Ian flexed his wrists a couple of times. Suddenly, without taking a practice swing, he swept his club back, twisting it behind his own head (he would have hit Friday right between the eyes if she hadn't moved).

Then he whipped the club through, smacking it into the ball with a crisp crack.

The ball shot into the sky with the speed of a bullet. They all shaded their eyes to follow its trajectory. It flew on and on, eventually dropping down about 220 metres away in the middle of the fairway. There was backspin on the ball, so it only bounced twice in the same spot before coming to rest.

Tom sighed. 'I'll never be that good.'

'How do you hit it so hard without looking like you're trying to hit it hard?' asked Stephan.

'The secret is talent, boys,' said Ian. 'I can't explain how I have so much of it.'

'Please don't try,' said Friday. 'I'm nauseous enough as it is.'

Ian smirked as he bent over to pick up his golf bag. 'I'll be on my way, then.' He turned to walk out to his ball, when suddenly something moved out of the tree line.

'What was that?!' exclaimed Tom.

Friday shaded her eyes and peered into the distance. '*Corvus corone*,' she said.

'I beg your pardon?' asked Stephan.

'It's a crow,' said Friday.

The big black bird flapped a few times, then glided out over the rolling grass of the fairway before landing neatly alongside Ian's ball. It picked up the ball in its beak.

'Do you see that?' exclaimed Tom.

'It's stealing my ball!' cried Ian.

Chapter 11

Binoculars

The crow stood on the fairway with the golf ball in its mouth for a moment.

'It must be a really hungry bird,' said Melanie.

'It must think it's an egg,' said Friday. 'Large birds often eat the eggs of other birds.'

Suddenly the crow leapt up into the air and flew off, taking the golf ball with it.

'Look at that!' said Friday. 'I bet that's what happened when you were playing the other day. The bird picked up your ball and dropped it closer to the hole. It's fascinating to observe.'

'It's not fascinating – that bird is going to ruin my score!' said Ian. 'Come back with my ball!' He started running down the fairway towards the bird, but he couldn't run as fast as the bird could fly.

Friday took off running as well. But she headed for the trees. She was running towards the point where the bird had first appeared above the tree line. Melanie followed after her, but at an amble that could barely be considered a jog. Tom and Stephan chased after Ian, because he was their golf idol, and they were more interested in helping him than assisting their own private detective.

When Friday ran into the trees, she was soon slowed down by the longer grass and undergrowth. She almost ran face-first into a statue of Hercules, which she noted was strangely enough wearing a nose ring. But then Friday saw a flash of movement up ahead and she ploughed through the undergrowth in that direction. She heard the squawk of the bird. It must have dropped the ball if it was squawking. Friday hurried faster. She could see now. There was a boy in the trees frantically trying to get the bird into a cage.

'Get in there,' the boy muttered at the bird. Then the bird must have pecked him because he recoiled. 'Ow!'

Friday ran full tilt at him, leaping forward and grabbing him in a crash tackle. The boy staggered for a couple of steps then steadied himself with Friday still wrapped around his waist. He was taller than her and a lot stockier, so she hadn't had enough force to knock him off his feet.

'Get off!' he cried.

'No, release that bird,' demanded Friday.

'It's my bird,' protested the boy.

'Then release the golf ball,' insisted Friday.

'Fine. It's just one golf ball,' said the boy. He took the ball out of his pocket and tossed it on the ground.

Friday realised she actually had no interest in the golf ball, so she wasn't going to let go of him to pick it up. 'What on earth are you doing?' she asked.

'None of your business, let me go!' cried the boy.

At that moment both of them were knocked off their feet. Ian had flung himself through the bushes and crash-tackled them. So Friday found herself at the bottom of a sort-of-violent, very scratchy group hug as she lay in the scrub beneath the two strug-gling boys.

'The ball is over there,' yelled the boy. 'Just take it!'

But Ian had him by the scruff of his collar. 'What are you doing? Did my father send you? Is this some sort of plot?'

'I don't know what you're talking about,' said the boy.

'Let him go,' said Friday to Ian. 'This has nothing to do with you.'

Ian looked at Friday. He could see she meant it, so he released the boy's collar.

'Thank you,' said the boy.

But at that moment Tom and Stephan came bursting through the undergrowth and crash-tackled the boy themselves.

'What is it with you nutty private school kids?' said the boy. 'Just get off me!'

'How much did he pay you to rig our game?' Stephan demanded.

'I've got no idea what you're talking about,' said the boy.

'Tell him I've never seen you before in my life,' insisted Tom.

'Let him go!' demanded Friday. 'He didn't fix your game.'

'Then what is he doing with that crazy ball-stealing bird?' demanded Ian.

'Look,' said Friday, pointing to the boy's equipment. There was a large bird cage and a canvas bag sitting on the ground. The canvas bag was full of golf balls.

'What is he doing with all those balls?' asked Stephan. 'Is it some sort of weird extreme sport that you play with a crow?'

'This boy is stealing golf balls for the sake of stealing golf balls,' said Friday.

'Why would anybody do that?' asked Tom.

Friday rolled her eyes. 'The reason why most people steal things – for the money, of course.'

'That's ridiculous,' said Tom. 'How much could you possibly get for a golf ball? A dollar a piece?'

'Exactly,' said Friday. 'He's got about sixty balls in that bag. That's $60.'

Tom and Stephan still looked confused.

'To normal kids,' said Friday, 'that is a lot of money.'

'Ooooh,' said Tom and Stephan, the penny finally beginning to drop.

'So you were stealing balls to get money to buy some sort of illicit contraband that poor people like?' asked Tom.

'I'm saving up to buy a bicycle,' said the boy.

'You have to buy your own? How extraordinary,' said Stephan.

'And you trained a crow?' asked Ian.

'I found her by the side of the road,' said the boy. 'She'd been hit by a car, so I looked after her until she could fly again. But she didn't want to fly away, she stayed close. One day she flew home with a golf ball and I realised she liked collecting things that looked like eggs. I started bringing her out here to look for lost balls. The rich kids don't bother looking for them if they go in the bushes, they just take out another ball and keep playing. But then she started grabbing balls right off the fairway.'

Ian laughed. 'It's not like this school to have such a simple crime as theft for theft's sake.'

'It's barely theft,' argued the boy. 'Most of the balls we find have been long abandoned. Here, there's your ball back.' The boy picked up the ball and handed it back to Ian.

'Thank you,' said Ian.

'So why did your crow drop his ball right by the hole?' asked Stephan.

'She often drops them,' said the boy. 'It's not easy holding a ball in a beak, you know. It was just luck that the ball landed so close to the hole.'

'So it was luck, after all,' said Tom happily. 'I won fair and square.'

'You can't let a bird interfere with your ball,' protested Stephan.

'I bet there's nothing in the rule book about crows carrying golf balls,' said Tom cheerfully. 'It's just the luck of the game.'

'Perhaps you'd better try another golf course for a while,' suggested Friday, turning to the boy, 'until you can train your crow to leave the balls in play alone.'

'I will,' said the boy. 'This school is too nutty for me. It's stressful. If students aren't crash-tackling me, then there's men with binoculars nabbing my best spot to spy on the school.'

'What?' said Friday. 'You've seen men in these woods watching the school with binoculars?'

Chapter 12

▰▰▰▰▰▰▰▰▰▰▰▰▰▰▰▰▰▰▰

The Red Sports Car

After several days, Friday's headache eased. But as her thinking cleared, she was beginning to puzzle more and more about the artfully vandalised artworks that kept turning up. Just the previous day the poster of Andy Warhol's 'Campbell's Soup Can' that decorated Mrs Marigold's kitchen had been altered. No one except Mrs Marigold and the Headmaster knew in what way the picture had changed, but the rumour was that the soup variety on the label was now very rude.

Friday and Melanie were ambling towards their maths lesson when they could distinctly hear yelling.

'Is that coming from the staff car park?' asked Friday.

'It sounds like it,' said Melanie.

'We should investigate,' said Friday.

'It could be someone dangerous,' said Melanie.

'I'd rather confront someone dangerous than listen to Miss Emerson drone on about quadratic equations,' said Friday. 'I like few equations more, but she still manages to make them boring.'

The girls hurried around the back of the maths classrooms towards the car park.

'Unchain it at once!'

'That sounds like Mr Maclean,' said Friday.

Mr Maclean was the geography master. He was not the best teacher at Highcrest, although he was certainly the vainest.

As the girls rounded the corner they saw a tow truck lifting the rear end of a shiny red sports car.

'You can't take my car!' protested Mr Maclean. 'I paid for it in full.'

'You should have checked to see if there was any money owing on it before you made the purchase,' said the tow-truck driver.

'I did!' exclaimed Mr Maclean. 'I ran it through the motor registry database.'

'Then you must have entered the plate number wrong,' said the tow-truck driver. 'It's definitely not yours. Checking that a car is owned in full by the seller is one of the key steps in purchasing a car. I have a leaflet explaining the details, if that would help.'

'I did check!' yelled Mr Maclean.

Friday went over and inspected the number plate. It would have been easy to misread. It was filthy and it looked like it had been run over. The number plate was flat when it should have been raised and lumpy around the edges. Even so, the lettering was legible. It read DAB 071. Friday fished a piece of notepaper and a pencil out of her bag.

'What are you doing?' asked Melanie.

'I'm taking a rubbing of the plate,' said Friday, 'before it gets towed away. They're too busy arguing. They won't mind.' She held the paper over the number plate, lay her pencil against the paper at an acute angle and ran it back and forth.

'Sir, there's no need to take that tone with me,' said the tow-truck driver. 'I'm just doing my job.'

'But it's not my fault,' said Mr Maclean. 'You should take this up with the seller.'

'No,' said the tow-truck driver. 'It's my job to reclaim the car because it hasn't been paid for. The fact that you are in possession of the car is irrelevant. You don't own it, because the person you bought it from didn't own it. Their bank did. And the bank wants it back.'

'But what about my money?' cried Mr Maclean.

You could understand his concern. Teaching is not the most lucrative profession.

'That's between you and the person you gave the money to,' said the tow-truck driver as he jumped into his cab and started to slowly drive away, the beautiful red sports car in tow.

'But I need that car!' wailed Mr Maclean. 'I'm taking Miss Priddock on a date tomorrow night.'

'I thought you weren't allowed to be romantically involved with a member of the support staff?' said Friday.

Mr Maclean spun on his heel and glared at Friday.

'I'm going to help her study for her first-aid course,' said Mr Maclean.

'You see yourself as a CPR dummy, do you?' asked Friday.

'I'm reporting you to the Headmaster!' yelled Mr Maclean.

'Really?' said Friday. 'Are you going to tell him about the sports car you bought with cash and the date with Miss Priddock, as well?'

'I've been swindled,' said Mr Maclean. 'You're the detective. I'm going to hire you to get to the bottom of it.'

'Whoa, there,' said Friday. 'I'm not agreeing to take the case.'

'I paid $10,000 for that car,' said Mr Maclean. 'If you can recover the money, I'll give you ten per cent.'

'I'm not good at mathematics,' said Melanie, 'but even I can work out that's $1000.'

'It is?' said Mr Maclean. 'Gosh, I meant to say $100.'

'Good luck,' said Friday, turning to go to her next class.

'All right, $1000,' said Mr Maclean. 'You can have a thousand if you get my money back.'

'Who did you buy the car from?' asked Friday.

'Mr Brecht,' said Mr Maclean.

'Oh dear,' said Melanie. 'He's probably spent it all on cheese by now.'

'Let's go and see him,' said Friday.

Friday, Melanie and Mr Maclean trudged down to the art classroom. They found Mr Brecht hunched over a linocut.

'I'm busy,' said Mr Brecht, without even looking up.

'Good, we're busy too,' said Friday. 'So let's not delay this process any further. Mr Maclean would like you to give him his $10,000 back, because the car you sold him has just been repossessed.'

'What? But I don't have the money anymore!' said Mr Brecht.

'Cheese?' asked Melanie.

'I gave it to Mrs Cannon,' said Mr Brecht.

'That dreadful woman!' exclaimed Mr Maclean.

'Yes, she is dreadful, isn't she?' said Mr Brecht with a grin. 'That's what I like about her. And she gave me some excellent advice.'

'About teaching?' asked Friday.

'Some of it was,' said Mr Brecht.

'Why did you give her all that money?' asked Friday.

'I bought her station wagon,' said Mr Brecht. 'I wanted a car with more storage space.'

'And that cost $10,000?' asked Friday.

'That's the going rate for a five-year-old station wagon with low mileage,' said Mr Brecht.

'Give me the car!' yelled Mr Maclean. 'You bought it with my money!'

'I will not,' said Mr Brecht. 'I've got a date with Miss Priddock tonight.'

'But I've got a date with her tomorrow night,' said Mr Maclean.

'I wouldn't be surprised if she cancels after a night out with me,' said Mr Brecht. 'Women are more attracted to great artists than they are to geology teachers.'

'Geography!' yelled Mr Maclean. 'I teach geography!'

'Is there a difference?' asked Mr Brecht.

'Yes,' said Friday.

'Although not much,' said Melanie. 'They can both be equally boring.'

'I'm going to report you to the police!' said Mr Maclean. 'You sold me a car with money still owed on it.'

'I didn't know that,' said Mr Brecht. 'I bought it with cash myself.'

'Where from?' asked Friday.

'The side of the road,' said Mr Brecht. 'It had a sign in the window saying, "Car for Sale". So I called the number and bought the car.'

'Didn't you check with the motor registry database to see if it was really owned by the seller?' asked Friday.

'No,' said Mr Brecht. 'The fellow seemed honest enough.'

'Well, he wasn't!' yelled Mr Maclean.

'I'm sorry for your trouble, Maclean,' said Mr Brecht, 'but it's not my problem. There's nothing I can do to help.'

'You could stop lying for a start,' said Friday.

'I beg your pardon?' said Mr Brecht.

'You knew exactly what you were doing when you sold Mr Maclean your car,' said Friday. 'The only reason it didn't turn up when he ran the number plate through the database was because you, an expert painter, had carefully changed the number plate.'

'Rubbish,' said Mr Brecht.

'The number plate on the car being towed away outside reads DAB 071,' said Friday. 'It would be so easy to change an "L" to a "D". Especially for an accomplished artist such as yourself.'

'You can't prove it,' said Mr Brecht.

'Yes, I can,' said Friday, 'because the letters on a number plate aren't just painted on – they're embossed into the metal. The metal is also moulded into the shape of each letter. You did a lovely job on ageing and battering the number plate so that it was hard to notice, but that in itself was suspicious. Why have an immaculate antique car and a beaten-up number plate, unless you're trying to hide something? So I took a rubbing of the plate. And only the raised embossing showed up.'

Friday held up her rubbing. It read LAB 071.

'It was a personalised plate, wasn't it?' said Friday. 'LAB are your initials. Was 1971 the year you were born?'

'Fine,' said Mr Brecht. 'But it's still not my problem. It's Mr Maclean's problem, because when you're buying a second-hand it's buyer beware.'

'What?' said Mr Maclean.

'Didn't it ever occur to you that $10,000 was incredibly cheap for an antique sports car?' said Mr Brecht.

'Well, yes, but I thought it was a bargain,' said Mr Maclean.

'You thought I was an idiot,' said Mr Brecht.

'Well, you are an art teacher,' said Mr Maclean.

'You got to drive the car for ten days,' said Mr Brecht. 'Think of that as a $1000 a day rental fee.'

'I'd never pay that much just to rent a car,' said Mr Maclean.

'Which is why gorgeous women like Miss Priddock will never find you attractive,' said Mr Brecht. 'Now get out of my classroom. If you want to contact the police, please do. You'll never get any money out of me because you paid in cash, and you never asked me to sign a receipt or any paperwork.'

'You're taking advantage of my good nature,' said Mr Maclean.

'Yes, I am,' agreed Mr Brecht. 'So, in addition to ten days rental of a lovely sports car, I've also given you a priceless lesson on not trusting strangers.'

'I'll tell the Headmaster,' said Mr Maclean.

'Go ahead,' said Mr Brecht. 'But Miss Priddock has shown me some of the love poetry you've sent her, and apart from being grossly inappropriate they could be used as evidence of your mental instability. So, on the whole, I suggest the wisest course of action would be to keep your mouth shut.'

Mr Maclean looked like he wanted to cry. He stalked off, slamming the door as he went.

'Did you want something, girls?' Mr Brecht asked, turning to Friday and Melanie.

'You swindled Mr Maclean,' said Friday. It was an accusation, but a very polite accusation. As though she couldn't believe the specimen she was observing under a microscope.

'Yes,' said Mr Brecht. 'You wouldn't believe how many times I've been swindled by agents, galleries and lawyers. This is a dog-eat-dog world. I make no claim to be a good person. I'm an artist. We're notorious for being dreadful.'

Mr Brecht went back to working on his lino cut. He clearly felt that the conversation was over.

'That was interesting,' said Friday as she and Melanie wandered back to their next class.

'Yes,' agreed Melanie, 'I like Mr Brecht. But I can't help feeling I shouldn't.'

'Exactly,' said Friday. 'Who knows what else he's capable of.'

Chapter 13

Fitness Tracking

It was a well-established fact that PE was Friday's least favourite subject. (The only person who disliked it more was Melanie.) Friday could intellectually see that it would be beneficial to be good at throwing, catching and running around. She was simply terrible at them, having no natural ability for anything that required coordination.

Melanie, on the other hand, may well have been capable of some athletic endeavour. She was tall, long-legged and slim, and her brothers had all done well at rugby and rowing. But no one would ever know, because the only thing that Melanie was adamantly determined about in life was that she would never engage in any athletic pursuit.

As you can imagine, this did not endear the two girls to their PE teacher. It was hard enough teaching sport and exercise at a school where all the students were so wealthy and privileged they thought they were above having to do anything. And if any of them were talented at a sport they had expert tuition at home and felt the school's teachers had nothing to offer them. On the whole, the students at Highcrest Academy preferred sports like polo, because a horse carried you around, or golf, because a caddy carried your bag around. Anything that involved the students not having to carry things was just fine.

Their total lack of discipline infuriated Mr Fontana, the new PE teacher. Friday had wondered if he would one day snap and try using a student as a javelin, but when he did snap it was in an entirely different way.

The students in Friday's class were all sitting on the floor of the gymnasium outside the PE staff room, waiting for their lesson to begin, when Mr Fontana emerged from his office carrying a large cardboard box. He walked onto the court, put down the box and addressed the group.

As per usual, the students didn't bother to stop talking amongst themselves. They rarely showed respect for the teachers they actually respected, so they were unlikely to show respect to a PE teacher. Mr Fontana sighed, walked over to the light switch on the wall and flicked it on and off several times with the back of his knuckles.

'Is-anybody-list-en-ing-to-me?' asked Mr Fontana, in syncopation with his flicking.

The students finally fell silent.

'Why would you flick the light switch on and off like that?' asked Friday.

'If any of us were epileptic, we might have a fit,' said Melanie.

'None of you are epileptic,' asked Mr Fontana. 'If you were, it would have been on your admission forms and I would have been told about it.'

'I'm more curious why you would flick the lights on and off with the back of your knuckle, instead of your finger,' said Friday.

'Would you all just be quiet? I'd like to start the lesson at some stage today,' said Mr Fontana.

The group hushed.

'As you know,' continued Mr Fontana, 'I think you are all shamefully lazy. It sickens me to look at your blank apathetic faces, let alone watch you listlessly perform any one of the proud sports I have tried to teach you.'

'Yes, you've mentioned these things several times,' agreed Melanie. 'If you don't enjoy your career in teaching, you should seriously consider getting a job in de-motivational speaking. You have quite the talent for it.'

'Pelly . . .' said Mr Fontana.

'Shut up?' asked Melanie.

'Yes,' said Mr Fontana. They had had many similar conversations before. 'Before we get into today's lesson on frizbee soccer . . .'

The class groaned.

'Frizbee soccer is a growing sport internationally, played by thousands of people every weekend because they think it's fun!' yelled Mr Fontana.

The class stared at the ground. They were used to these fits of temper. They would always pass if they ignored them. Mr Fontana was not really meant to yell at students like that – he knew it and the students knew it. But they had formed a symbiotic relationship, where they would behave terribly and he would throw tantrums but no one would ever take it any further. What happened in PE, stayed in PE.

'Your complete lack of respect for any formal sport aside,' continued Mr Fontana, 'I know that many of you are vain and narcissistic –'

'What's narcissistic?' asked Mirabella.

'Look in the mirror,' said Ian.

'And see what?' asked Mirabella.

'A classic example of narcissism,' said Friday. 'Narcissus was so enchanted by his own reflection in a pond that –'

'Would you all just –' began Mr Fontana.

'Shut up,' chanted the class in unison.

'Yes,' continued Mr Fontana. 'Since you are all so concerned with your appearance, I thought one way to make you interested in your own fitness would be to show you just how lazy you are and that – if you continued in your slack, sedentary ways, consuming the amount of calories you do – you will soon become overweight, pimple-ridden, weak-boned husks of human beings.'

'I can't follow what he's saying,' said Mirabella. 'He's using too many big words.'

'He's saying you'll get fat and ugly if you don't exercise,' said Friday.

'How dare you!' yelled Mirabella. 'I'm calling Daddy, you can't say that to me.'

'Yes, I can,' said Mr Fontana. 'I'm going to statistically prove that I'm right –' he picked up his large box and tipped the contents out on the floor '– with these.' Thirty small boxes tumbled out.

'What are they?' asked Friday.

'Fitness trackers,' said Mr Fontana. 'You wear them on your wrist.' He was already wearing one, and held up his arm to show the class. 'They measure the number of steps you take, your heart rate, the amount of sleep you get, and how many kilometres you walk.'

'Cool,' said Ian, opening up a box and trying a tracker on.

'You can't expect us to wear those!' exclaimed Mirabella. 'They're so ugly!'

'Tough,' said Mr Fontana.

'How exactly do they measure the number of kilometres we've walked?' asked Friday.

'With GPS technology,' said Mr Fontana. 'Your exact location is tracked by a satellite, then the information is sent back and stored in your tracker, as well as on my computer in my office.'

'Then I'm afraid I have to agree with Mirabella,' said Friday. 'You can't expect us to wear those. It's a complete invasion of our privacy.'

'What are you talking about?' demanded Mr Fontana. 'I'm just going to use them to prove how lazy and idle you all are.'

'Yes, but by tracking our movements twenty-four hours a day,' protested Friday.

'Do you have something to hide, Friday?' asked Ian.

'That's none of your business,' said Friday. 'That's none of anybody's business. That's what privacy means.'

'You're a high-school student,' said Mr Fontana. 'You have no right to privacy.'

'I don't think that's true,' said Friday. 'Where did all these trackers come from anyway? They must have been expensive.'

'They were donated by an anonymous benefactor,' said Mr Fontana.

'Who?' asked Friday.

'I knew you lot would cause trouble,' said Mr Fontana, taking a folded piece of paper out of his pocket, 'so I had the Headmaster write a letter of authority for me.' Mr Fontana shook out the letter and began to read:

'Dear students,

Every one of you, in every grade, will wear these wrist trackers for the duration of the one-month trial. That is an order. Directly from me, your headmaster.

I don't want to hear any complaints from anybody about it, especially you, Friday Barnes. The students at this school are woefully inadequate at just about every academic standard. The least you can do is the bare minimum of physical exertion so that you don't succumb to low blood pressure or bed sores while you are still students here at Highcrest Academy.

So put the devices on now. That is an order. Anyone caught taking off their tracker for any reason other than having a shower will be disciplined with the punishment of Mr Fontana's choice, which I'm sure will involve a deeply unpleasant amount of a repetitive exercise.

Yours sincerely, the Headmaster.'

'What's the deeply unpleasant exercise?' asked Ian.

'One hundred burpees,' said Mr Fontana. 'Anyone who takes their tracker off will have to report here each morning before breakfast and do one hundred burpees.'

Friday stood up. Mr Fontana held out a tracker to her. She looked at the box but did not take it. 'The reason I am standing up is so I can begin my burpees,' said Friday.

'What?' said Mr Fontana.

'I refuse to put that tracker on,' said Friday. 'I will not allow this school to electronically monitor my every movement like I am a package from Amazon or a prisoner on weekend detention. I will take the one-hundred-burpees option.'

'But, Friday,' said Melanie, 'that's one hundred burpees every day for a month!'

'Some things are worth sacrificing for,' said Friday. She stepped out in front of the group. 'Should I begin?'

'Go ahead,' said Mr Fontana.

'Right,' said Friday. 'Who will join me in refusing to wear the tracker, and instead doing burpees?'

The class had already passed the trackers out amongst themselves.

'I think it's cool,' said Harris, playing with the buttons on the tracker. 'Look, it can read my heart.'

'I wanted one of these for Christmas,' added Trea. 'My sister's always going on about how many steps she takes. Now I can totally smoke her.'

'No one?' asked Friday. She looked at Melanie.

Melanie shook her head. 'Sorry, I'd rather spend all day walking around wearing a webcam with live internet streaming attached to my forehead than do even one burpee.'

'You're on your own, Barnes,' said Ian.

'Fine,' said Friday. She took a deep breath ready to begin, then turned to Mr Fontana. 'What's a burpee again?'

Mr Fontana sighed and shook his head. 'You lie

down flat on your stomach, get back up, jump and clap your hands over your head.'

'You're kidding?' said Friday.

'No,' said Mr Fontana shaking his head.

Friday gritted her teeth and reconciled herself to the task. She put her hands down on the floor, stepped her legs back and lay down on her chest. That wasn't too bad. Then she got back up, jumped and clapped her hands over her head.

'One,' said Mr Fontana.

'One?' said Friday. 'But there were four different movements there.'

'I know what a burpee is,' said Mr Fontana. 'And that is just one of them. You've got ninety-nine more to go.'

Chapter 14

Mural

Friday and Melanie were sitting in the art classroom waiting for Mr Brecht. Friday had never hurt so much in her life. She'd expected her arms and legs to be achy, but her stomach muscles felt traumatised, and even though she'd been doing the burpees on grass, the pitch was pretty dry and she'd managed to take the skin off both knees.

'I always knew exercise was deeply unpleasant,' said Friday, 'but I never knew just how deeply unpleasant until today.'

'And to think, some people do it voluntarily,' said Melanie. 'They even claim to enjoy it.'

'Ugh,' said Mr Brecht as he stomped up the stairs into the classroom and slapped his satchel down on his desk.

He was twenty minutes late.

'Problem, sir?' asked Melanie.

'Your idiot of a headmaster has given me an assignment,' complained Mr Brecht.

'Are you allowed to call the headmaster an idiot?' asked Melanie.

'One of the advantages of being on a short-term contract is that the process of firing me would take longer than just letting me serve out my contract,' said Mr Brecht. 'As a result, I can say just what I like, about just who I like.'

'I'm not sure that's entirely true,' said Friday. 'If you said you murdered someone, I'm pretty sure the Headmaster would fire you straight away.'

'If he found out,' said Melanie. 'Lots of things go on at this school without the Headmaster ever finding out.'

'True,' agreed Friday. 'Like all the weird graffiti that keeps popping up on pictures around the school.

Look at the Mona Lisa behind you. There's a perfectly executed Renaissance style depiction of an airplane flying behind her head.'

'Would you two shut up so we can find out what Mr Brecht is going on about?' snapped Ian. 'That is actually interesting, unlike anything either of you has to say.'

'The Headmaster isn't content with humiliating me by making me teach children,' said Mr Brecht.

'You mean, doing your job?' said Friday.

'Precisely,' said Mr Brecht. 'It is mortifying for an artist of my calibre to be reduced to this.'

'So why don't you quit?' asked Friday. 'Surely you could arrange some sort of payment scheme with the tax department?'

'Humph!' grumbled Mr Brecht. 'The tax department is the least of my worries. No, the Headmaster knows I can't escape, so now he's making me arrange this stupid art show.'

'I thought that was meant to highlight your inspirational influence on the students' artwork?' said Melanie.

'As if I want that highlighted!' said Mr Brecht. 'The fewer people who know I've been reduced to "teaching", the better.' He said the word 'teaching' as if it was the worst swear word he had ever said. 'But, to add insult to injury, he's asked me to design a mural.'

'A urinal?' asked Patel, who was sitting in the back row and as such couldn't hear clearly.

'No, although I'd enjoy that more,' said Mr Brecht. 'At least designing a urinal, or any sort of toilet, really, would be an artistic challenge. No, I have to have my nose ground into my humiliation, by designing a blasted great big mural that will stand for all posterity on a wall of this school.'

'Which wall?' asked Friday.

'The northern wall of the science block,' said Mr Brecht.

'But that's huge!' said Friday. 'It's a two-storey building, so it must be at least six metres high and thirty metres long. The mural would be 180 square metres!'

'It would?' exclaimed Mr Brecht. 'Urgh, I really wish you hadn't done the mathematics, Barnes. Now I'm even more depressed.'

'Sorry, sir,' said Friday.

'The whole thing is just so utterly boring it makes me want to vomit,' said Mr Brecht.

'You really do have an artistic temperament, don't you, sir?' said Melanie.

'On the bright side, being an idiot, the Headmaster has given me a ridiculously inflated budget,' said Mr Brecht, 'which means if we're going to desecrate a great big wall with the amateur scrawlings of this student body, at least we can do it properly.'

'What do you mean by "properly"?' asked Ian. 'Are you thinking spatter painting like Jackson Pollock? Will we be using cannons?'

'No, we will not,' said Mr Brecht. 'I may be this country's leading avant-garde artist, but I still believe a painting should look like something.'

'So how are you spending your huge budget?' asked Friday.

'On cheese?' asked Melanie.

'No, although that's not a bad idea,' said Mr Brecht, 'I am peckish. No, I'm getting a building company to come in and erect scaffolding across the entire face of the building so we can cover every last inch with paint.'

'Cool,' said Peregrine.

'And it has the added benefit of minimising the chance of anyone plummeting to their death,' said

Mr Brecht. 'This job is bad enough without me having to fill in endless tedious Occupational Health and Safety forms just because some student is too stupid to not know how to hang out of a window without dying.'

'What will the mural depict?' asked Friday.

Mr Brecht grinned. 'I'm not telling anyone. Because whatever I decide, there would be some committee discussion about it, with tie-wearing nerds telling me how I could "improve" my work. Then I'd probably strangle someone and get in real trouble. So, to save myself from that, I'm just not going to tell anyone.'

'Aren't the students meant to do the painting?' asked Ian.

'Yes,' said Mr Brecht.

'So how does that work?' asked Ian. 'Will we paint wearing blindfolds?'

'That wouldn't be very safe up on a scaffold,' said Melanie.

'No, my plan is much more brilliant than that,' said Mr Brecht. 'I've done my design, and I've cut it up into 350 pieces, one for each student at this school. The pieces are numbered. Each student will have to take their ten centimetre by ten centimetre piece and enlarge it in a numbered square on the building.'

'Like a colour-by-numbers painting?' asked Friday.

'Yes,' said Mr Brecht, 'like a giant colour-by-numbers painting where you each only get one number.'

'It sounds more interesting than the macramé plant hangers Miss Van Den Porten had us make in art last term,' said Ian.

Mr Brecht rifled through his satchel and pulled out a big plastic bag. 'Here, you lot can get the first pieces. Line up down the middle of the room, then take your turns pulling a piece of the design out of this bag.'

The class lined up. Because she was sitting in the front row, and everyone lined up behind her, Melanie was at the front of the line. She reached into the plastic bag and pulled out a small square of paper. Melanie looked at it.

'It's just blue,' said Melanie.

'Lucky you,' said Mr Brecht. 'That will be nice and easy for you to paint.'

'Thank you,' said Melanie, smiling happily.

Friday reached in next. She pulled out a design that was a sort of pink and black swirl. 'Mine looks like a snail shell,' said Friday.

'You're a talented artist,' said Mr Brecht, 'I'm sure you can handle the challenge.'

And so the process continued until each person in the class had a design. Patel was considered the next luckiest after Melanie because all he had on his design was a big round black circle. Ian had a more challenging part of the design that looked like zebra stripes. But most people got variations on pink, brown, blue or black blobs.

'I can't believe he gets paid for this,' muttered Mirabella. 'He's some fancy-pants artist, but my four-year-old sister could come up with something more interesting.'

'Really?' said Melanie. 'It's nice to know that someone in your family is talented.'

Friday stared at the design in her hand.

'What's wrong?' asked Melanie.

'I don't know,' said Friday. 'But I'm sure something is.'

Chapter 15

▰▰▰▰▰▰▰▰▰▰▰▰▰▰▰▰▰

Abduction

One week later, Friday and Melanie were sitting up on the scaffolding alongside the science block. It had only taken them a few minutes to paint their sections of the mural, and now they were enjoying their elevated view over the school. Friday was staring at the sky observing some particularly interesting *Cumulus humilis* clouds (white fluffy ones) when Melanie spotted something.

'Why do you think Marcus Welby is running away from those two men in suits?' asked Melanie.

Friday didn't have as good eyesight as Melanie, so she peered in the direction that her friend was pointing. She soon spotted Marcus's red hair as he weaved between the admin building and the music rooms. 'He certainly seems to be in a hurry. Let's climb down and see what's going on.'

Friday and Melanie had just scrambled down to ground level, when Marcus appeared on the far side of the quadrangle.

'Friday!' cried Marcus, as he sprinted towards her. 'You've got to help me! Please!'

He skidded to a halt, grabbing hold of a picnic table and trying to hide himself behind Friday and Melanie, which was foolish because he was unusually tall for a year 8 boy with red hair, so two normal-sized girls did not provide adequate cover.

Two men in suits now appeared on the far side of the quadrangle. They spotted Marcus and started running towards him.

'Don't let them take me!' wailed Marcus.

'Who are they?' asked Friday.

'The police,' said Marcus.

'What did you do?' asked Friday.

'Nothing!' protested Marcus.

'Grab him!' cried the slower of the two police officers.

Friday stood up and blocked his way. 'Wait one minute,' she said. 'I will not allow you to grab him.'

'Get out of the way, kid!' growled the police officer. He stepped forward as if to shove his way past Friday.

'Hold on!' cried the Headmaster. He was hurrying across the quadrangle to join the group.

'Why are you arresting him?' asked Friday.

'We don't have to answer your questions!' snapped the older police officer.

'They say a boy matching Marcus Welby's description was seen vandalising a car in Stratham last night,' panted the Headmaster.

'And you're arresting him for this crime?' asked Friday.

The police officers glanced at each other. 'We're taking him in for questioning,' said the older police officer.

'Unless you arrest him, Marcus doesn't have to go with you,' said Friday.

'I don't want to be arrested!' cried Marcus.

'Yes, you do,' said Friday. 'If you are arrested, then

you are protected by certain legal rights. They must take you before a magistrate, they can only hold you for a certain amount of time and they have to allow you to contact a lawyer. If they persuade you into "going in for questioning", you are not protected by any of those legal rights.'

'All right then, we'll arrest you,' said the older police officer. 'Marcus Welby, I am arresting you for vandalism. You have the right to remain silent. Anything you do or say can and will be used in a court of law.'

'The PTA is going to be so cross when they hear about this,' said the Headmaster. 'It's bad enough when staff get arrested, but now the students as well?'

The younger officer grabbed Marcus by the arm. 'Let's go.'

Friday grabbed Marcus by the other arm. 'Wait! Who are you?' she asked the officers.

'We're the police,' said the older police officer.

'Do you work with Sergeant Dowley?' asked Friday.

'Yes,' said the older police officer.

'That's strange, because the local police sergeant is called Sergeant Crowley,' said Friday.

153

'Then I misheard you,' said the older police officer. 'We know Crowley, he's a good man.'

'Sergeant Crowley is a woman,' said Friday.

'I mean, woman,' said the older police officer.

'No, he's actually a man,' said Friday. 'You've got nothing to do with the local police, have you?'

'All right, you've got us,' said the older police officer. 'We're not locals. We're part of a national vandalism task force.'

'Friday, we don't want you being arrested for police harassment as well,' said the Headmaster.

'Don't worry,' said Friday, 'that's not going to happen. Because these men aren't real police officers. Federal police don't deal with vandalism. Even local police are barely interested in it.'

'There's been a change in policy,' said the older police officer. 'A national crackdown.'

'Federal police do, however, know the correct wording to use when arresting a person,' said Friday. 'They don't just paraphrase what they've heard on TV cop shows. You told Marcus that anything he says "can and will be used against him in a court of law". You should have said, "*may* be used".'

'That doesn't make any difference,' said the older police officer.

'Yes it does,' said Friday. 'By saying "can and will", that means you have to tell a judge if he says, "I'd like a slice of pizza".'

'What are you saying?' asked the Headmaster.

'I don't know who these men are,' said Friday, 'but they are not police officers. And if they are trying to take Marcus with them, then they are trying to kidnap him.'

'Get the boy,' snarled the older police officer. 'We're getting out of here.'

The younger officer tightened his grip on Marcus and yanked him.

'Ow!' cried Marcus. 'My arm!'

The younger officer had pulled very hard on Marcus's arm. But what they had failed to notice was that Friday had handcuffed his other arm to the picnic table.

'Proper police officers also have handcuffs,' said Friday. 'Like my handcuffs, which I just used to attach Marcus to this table.'

'Barnes, why on earth are you carrying handcuffs with you?' asked the Headmaster.

'I always do,' said Friday. 'They're very useful.'

'Give me the key!' snapped the fake older police officer.

'Get it yourself,' said Friday, as she tossed the key up on the roof of the building. 'Go on, I'm sure Mr Pilcher will lend you a ladder. If you walk over to his shed and back, that'll only take you twenty minutes – which, coincidentally, is about how long it takes Sergeant Crowley to drive out here from the real police station.'

'Actually,' said the Headmaster, 'he should be here in ten minutes. I got Miss Priddock to make a call to him and the school's lawyer when these gentlemen first arrived.'

The two men looked at each other.

The school bell rang. Hundreds of students started streaming out into the quadrangle.

'Run!' the older man urged. They both sprinted through the crowd, knocking students down.

'Quick, Headmaster! They're trying to get away!' urged Friday. 'Give the order to close the front gate!'

'Gosh, yes!' said the Headmaster. He started running with Friday and Melanie back to the admin block. But the Headmaster wasn't good at moving quickly. The sea of milling students had grown larger. And he couldn't get away with knocking them over. By the time he finally reached the front office and stopped panting long enough to tell Miss Priddock to shut the gate, the two men were long gone.

'Never mind,' said Melanie. 'At least they didn't get to kidnap Marcus.'

'Marcus!' exclaimed Friday. 'He's still handcuffed to the picnic table!'

They all hurried back to release Marcus.

'Sorry, Marcus, we'll have you out in a jiffy,' said Friday.

'Don't you have to get the key down from the roof?' said the Headmaster.

'Gosh, no,' said Friday. 'I'll just put a sieve at the bottom of the downpipe and pick it up next time it rains. I've got a spare key I can use to let you out now.'

Friday released Marcus.

'Thank you so much,' said Marcus, rubbing his wrist. 'I was really scared.'

'The question remains, though,' said Friday. 'Why did those men want to kidnap you?'

'I don't know,' said Marcus. 'I've never done anything interesting in my life.'

'It's true,' said the Headmaster. 'He's a remarkably unremarkable student.'

'Could someone have tried to kidnap you to get at your parents?' asked Friday. 'Or at a rich relative who might pay a large ransom?'

'My family is rich,' said Marcus, 'but they're not that rich. If you were going to kidnap a student to get a ransom, there would be a couple of hundred kids here who would be better to choose. My mum makes her money from gravel mining. It's not a liquid asset. She wouldn't be able to get a lot of cash together quickly.'

'Environmentalists are getting increasingly militant,' said the Headmaster. 'Perhaps that had something to do with it.'

'Those two men did not look like environmentalists to me,' said Friday. 'They looked like hired thugs, which was why they were so convincing as police officers. There is something serious going on here. And perhaps a case of mistaken identity.'

Chapter 16

Breaking and Exiting

Two weeks had passed, and there had been no more attempts to kidnap Marcus Welby, or any other student for that matter. No more paintings had been vandalised and, surprisingly, Friday was actually getting better at doing burpees.

Friday had learned that it was a really bad idea to stop for a rest when you're lying on the ground, because it's very hard to summon the will to get up again from that position. She'd learned that it was better to not take rest breaks at all, because even after a rest the burpees still felt horrible, so it was better to get them over with. And she had learned that burpees weren't too bad for the first three, then they suddenly plunged into horribleness and stayed there for the remaining ninety-seven.

Mr Fontana had taken to placing a fitness tracker on the grass in front of Friday's nose as she lay down, to try and tempt her into taking the easy way out. He didn't really care if Friday wore the tracker or not, but he was fed up with having to spend twenty-five minutes of every morning watching her flail around on the ground and getting back up again.

Epstein was having to do burpees too. On the second day of the trial, his tracker had broken. He claimed it was an accident, but the dorm supervisor had seen him smash it with a brick. Epstein was much quicker than Friday at burpees. He actually jumped down and up again. And even though he was tall and lanky, the whole movement only took him a few seconds so the burpees were all done in just minutes. Friday took way longer.

She had been working for nearly twelve minutes and had only finished her forty-eighth burpee for the morning when a year 8 boy jogged down to the oval.

'Sir,' he said to Mr Fontana, 'the Headmaster wants to see Barnes.'

The crowd groaned. An increasingly large group had taken to gathering to watch Friday perform her daily exercise punishment. There were a lot of people who Friday had irritated and outright enraged during her time at Highcrest Academy. Not everyone enjoyed her crime-solving abilities, notably the people who had committed the crimes. And Ian Wainscott was positively delighted by the situation. Every morning, he would run a sweep-stake and take bets on how many burpees Friday would perform before she collapsed gasping, and how long it would take her to complete the whole number.

'She's only got fifty-two burpees to go,' said Mr Fontana.

'Fifty-one,' corrected Melanie. 'She did another one while you were talking.'

'He said now, sir,' said the boy.

'All right,' said Mr Fontana.

The crowd booed.

Friday smiled a very sweaty smile, and stopped mid-burpee.

'But you'll have to make them up by doing 151 tomorrow,' said Mr Fontana.

The crowd cheered.

Friday sighed and began following the boy back to the Headmaster's office, with Melanie in tow.

'What are you up to now?' asked the Headmaster as soon as Friday and Melanie stepped into his office. 'Or do I not want to know?'

Friday shook her head. 'Sorry, sir, I'm confused. I've just been forced to perform exercise, which is never good for my cognitive processes. What are you talking about?'

'If you're up to something illicit but that is somehow for the greater good, could you please do a better job of hiding it from me?!' said the Headmaster.

Friday turned to Melanie. 'Do you know what he's talking about?'

'No, but I never do,' said Melanie.

'May I sit down?' asked Friday. 'I'm a little light-headed.'

'No, you may not,' said the Headmaster. 'You're covered in sweat. Those are antique leather-upholstered chairs.'

'All right,' said Friday. 'Just explain: What is it you think I've done?'

'Breaking out of the school,' said the Headmaster.

'Why would I do that?' asked Friday.

'I don't know,' said the Headmaster. 'But you've done it before to go off mystery-solving. So what is it this time? Are you going to solve the Kennedy assassination? Or are you nipping off to Scotland to find the Loch Ness monster?'

'I'm not going anywhere,' said Friday.

'To the best of your knowledge,' qualified Melanie. 'You might be sleepwalking. And you have had multiple head injuries this term, so you could be doing things when you're concussed.'

'If I'd been sleepwalking, there would've been clues,' said Friday. 'Mud on the soles of my feet, dew-damp pyjamas and tiredness in my legs.'

'Do you have tired legs?' asked Melanie.

'Yes, but that's from all the burpees,' said Friday.

'Or is it?' asked Melanie, waggling her eyebrows.

'I'm sure I haven't been sleepwalking,' said Friday, turning to the Headmaster, who was the marginally more sensible person in the room.

'Then who has been breaking out? And why?' asked the Headmaster.

'I don't know,' said Friday. 'Are you sure it's not someone breaking in? Perhaps another kidnapping attempt?'

'Good grief, I hadn't even thought of that,' said the Headmaster, mopping his brow. 'But no students have gone missing, so I doubt it. I don't really want to know what is going on, but the culprit isn't doing a very good job of being covert. They keep cutting a hole in the perimeter fence. If someone is sneaking out and I don't know about it, then it's easy for me to say I don't know about it because I actually don't. But if someone is sneaking out and cutting holes in the fence, I can't say I don't know about it, because I know about the holes, and Mr Pilcher knows about them too because he's been complaining about having to keep fixing them. Which means I have to fill in paperwork and inform the school council and they'll expect me to put a stop to it.'

'Poor sir,' said Melanie.

'I want you to get to the bottom of this,' said the Headmaster. 'Find out who's cutting the holes.'

'And why?' asked Friday.

'Yes, I suppose I'll have to know that too,' said the Headmaster. 'Although I'd rather not. The things students do are bad enough. The reasons why they do them are positively horrifying.'

'And how will I be paid for this service?' asked Friday.

'What?!' exclaimed the Headmaster. 'Your tuition and board are already fully paid up for the next eighteen months. What more do you want? You can't squeeze blood from a stone.'

'I want the burpees to stop,' said Friday.

'Deal,' said the Headmaster. 'You get to the bottom of this, and I'll give you a full pardon from your punishment with Mr Fontana.'

Friday and Melanie walked out to the school's perimeter fence. The Headmaster had given them directions to find the area where the holes had repeatedly been cut. It was a long walk, across the rugby field, the polo pitch and through the woods, before they came to the section of fencing.

The fence around the school was nine feet high and was made of vertical steel bars with minimal cross-beams, like a pool fence, so that it was impossible to climb. It was very new and of the highest quality construction, having been built for the arrival of Princess Ingrid of Norway just a term and a half ago.

'There's the spot,' said Friday, pointing to a section where several of the bars had been bent back. She went over and crouched down to inspect it closely. 'It looks like they've been cut, but not with a saw, with some sort of crushing tool.'

'Like a pair of pliers?' asked Melanie.

'It would take a lot more than a pair of pliers to cut through one-inch-thick toughened steel bars,' said Friday. 'It must have been some sort of large pneumatic tool.'

'Is that a tool with pneumonia?' asked Melanie.

'No, pneumatic,' said Friday. 'It means air-powered, or more likely compressed-air-powered.'

Friday grabbed hold of one of the severed bars, and pulled it as hard as she could. It didn't budge. She leaned back, using all her weight to yank at the bar, but unfortunately the grass was damp, so she lost her footing and ended up landing flat on her back. 'It must have been bent back by a very strong tool as well.'

'To be fair,' said Melanie, 'a tool wouldn't have to be particularly strong to be stronger than you.'

'Let's see where they were going,' said Friday, as she crawled over to the hole, lay down on the grass and started to squeeze through.

'What are you doing?' said Melanie. 'You don't have permission to leave school grounds.'

'When has that ever stopped us before?' asked Friday, twisting round to look at Melanie as she snaked herself through the gap.

'It's just that when the Headmaster asked us to investigate the hole,' said Melanie, 'I don't think he expected us to use it ourselves.'

'We have to figure out where they were going,' said Friday, 'and we can't do that from inside of the fence.' She was now on her feet beyond the fence, in what was officially a national park. 'You're not scared of getting in trouble, are you?'

'No,' said Melanie. 'I just don't like it when things involve more exercise than I'd expected.' She begrudgingly got down on the ground and squeezed through the gap herself.

Friday was scanning the surrounding area. 'What do you see?' she asked.

'Is that a trick question?' asked Melanie, getting to her feet. 'All I can see is forest. But is it one of those mind-twisters, like not being able to see the forest for the trees?'

'No, all I can see is forest too,' said Friday. 'I'd expected there to be some sort of vehicle access. Otherwise, why cut through the fence here? I assumed that the person getting out was being met by a car.'

'Or a helicopter,' said Melanie.

'I think someone at the school would notice if a helicopter landed,' said Friday.

'Not if they did it when we were all in the school hall for assembly singing the national anthem,' said Melanie.

'There's nowhere for a helicopter to land amongst all these trees,' said Friday.

'It could be alien abduction,' said Melanie. 'They don't need to land their UFOs. They just use tractor beams to pull people up.'

'Are you speaking from personal experience?' asked Friday.

Melanie shook her head. 'If I have been abducted by aliens, they must have wiped my memory because I don't know anything about it. But then I don't know anything about algebra either, and I've been sitting in maths class every day for a year.'

'Two years,' said Friday. 'You're repeating year 7, remember?'

'Oh, yes,' said Melanie, 'I'd forgotten. The first time I did year 7 wasn't very interesting.'

'Anyway,' said Friday, 'even if I was to suspend all logic and pursue the hypothesis that this was alien abduction, that still wouldn't make any sense, because they could abduct the person from the inside of the fence and save the effort of having to cut a hole.'

'Brilliant, I hadn't thought of that,' said Melanie. 'And I guess if aliens do have the technology to travel through outer space and suck people up with tractor beams, then we have to assume that they are at least as intelligent as you.'

'You would hope so,' agreed Friday. 'Aliens would be bad enough, but silly aliens would be problematic. Let's see if we can find any non-alien footprints.'

'What do you want me to do?' asked Melanie.

'Stand still and don't make any footprints your-self,' said Friday.

'Oh, good,' said Melanie. 'I like standing still.'

Friday bent over and started systematically search-ing the ground near the hole in the fence.

'Do you see anything?' asked Melanie.

'Yes, the ground is perfect,' said Friday. 'There are lots of small animal tracks, rabbits and the like, and over here there are human footprints.' She started following a trail that was invisible to Melanie.

'What sort of shoes are they wearing?' asked Melanie.

'It's hard to tell,' said Friday. 'The grass doesn't leave a clear outline . . . Oh! Here we go, there's a footprint. That's odd . . .' Friday got down on her hands and knees and closely inspected the muddy mark on the ground.

'What is it?' called Melanie, who was dutifully standing still near the fence.

'Come and see,' called Friday. 'It looks like it was made by a lady's shoe.'

Melanie came over. The footprint was like the forefoot of a high-heel print, but it didn't look right. 'It's too big to fit a woman,' said Melanie.

'Unless it was a very large woman,' said Friday.

'Do we know any unusually large women?' asked Melanie.

'Not with large feet,' said Friday.

'Could the mud have expanded?' said Melanie. 'When it dried?'

'No, if anything, the reverse would happen,' said Friday. 'When mud dries it contracts.' She stood up and looked around. 'And where do they go? There are one, two, three clear footprints here in the mud, but then they disappear.'

'Look, there are some more,' said Melanie. 'On the other side of the tree.'

Friday went round to check. There were exactly the same footprints but this time going back the other way, towards the school.

'How very odd,' said Friday. 'It's as if someone has disappeared, then reappeared on this exact spot.'

'Wearing overly large women's shoes,' said Melanie. 'My money is still on the alien abduction.'

Friday turned slowly in a full circle, making note of everything she could observe. Then she stopped and gazed up. It was hard to observe anything because of the thick foliage of the tree's canopy. But just above her head height there was a branch. 'Look at this,' said Friday. 'The bark has been rubbed off right here.'

Melanie peered at the branch. 'What does that mean? That a beaver did it?'

Friday looked up at the canopy. 'No, I think someone has been climbing this tree. Give me a leg up.'

'I don't do leg-ups,' said Melanie firmly. 'We've discussed this before.'

Friday nodded. She respected her friend's principles. 'That's all right, I think I can do it.'

Friday grabbed hold of the branch and swung her legs up to the trunk then walked up the tree until her feet were level with the branch, where she hooked them over. She was now hanging on the underside of the branch like a sloth.

'Well done,' said Melanie. 'I never imagined you'd get that far. All those burpees must be paying off.'

Friday wiggled and scrambled until eventually she was scraped and sweaty but on the top side of the branch. She cautiously stood up, balancing herself against the trunk. Her head was lost inside the canopy now. 'I'm going to go a bit higher. It's easier now that the branches are closer together.' Friday disappeared into the canopy altogether.

Melanie could see nothing. She could just hear Friday awkwardly scrambling about through the foliage. 'If you do get abducted by aliens,' Melanie called, 'you will say something, won't you? I'd feel silly if I was standing here waiting for you, when you were halfway to Alpha Centauri.'

'Don't worry, I'm still earthbound,' Friday called down. 'But I've found something!'

'What?' asked Melanie.

'It's a flying fox!' said Friday.

'Don't touch it!' said Melanie. 'It might bite you.'

'Not the bat-type of flying fox,' said Friday, 'the rope-slide-type of flying fox.'

'They're almost as bad,' said Melanie. 'Tremendously dangerous, and so much hanging on.'

'I'm going to see where it goes,' said Friday.

'Are you sure that's wise?' asked Melanie.

The next moment, Friday came smashing out through the canopy. 'Whooopeee!' she cried as she was shooting down the guide rope at top speed into a gully.

'Friday!' cried Melanie.

'This is so much f–Oww!' cried Friday as she crashed loudly into a bush at the bottom of the rock face.

'Are you all right?' called Melanie.

'Not really,' said Friday. 'I would have been all right if I'd just hit the bush, but I appear to have landed on some sort of bicycle.'

'Really?' said Melanie. 'Is it a penny-farthing? Perhaps it's been there since the nineteenth century.'

Friday scrambled to her feet. 'No, it's modern and fancy-looking. I'm pretty sure it's what you'd call a mountain bike.'

'I'll take your word for it,' said Melanie. 'Any other clues?'

'I can see track marks,' said Friday. 'Someone has ridden the bike off into the forest, directly due north.'

'What's directly due north?' asked Melanie.

'Stratham,' said Friday. 'That's the nearest big town. They must have been heading there. If you go straight through the forest, it would be half the distance of going by road. On a bicycle, it would probably only take half an hour to get there.'

'You're not going to ride it there to see, are you?' asked Melanie.

'No,' said Friday. 'I'm not riding a bicycle on a flat surface, let alone in a forest, with so many trees to slam into. I'll come back up.'

But this was easier said than done. Friday soon realised why there was a flying fox to bridge the escarpment. The rock face was dangerously difficult to climb. She walked back and forth trying to figure out the best route, but there simply wasn't one.

'I think you're going to have to go back to school and get assistance,' said Friday.

'Really?' said Melanie. 'Okay. But would it help if I tossed this rope down to you?'

'What rope?' asked Friday.

'There's a neatly coiled rope right here at the top of the escarpment,' said Melanie. 'One end is tied to the tree.'

'Throw it over,' said Friday.

'Do you want me to untie it first?' asked Melanie.

'No!' cried Friday. 'Throw the loose end down. This must be the way our suspect climbs back up.'

'Oh, how clever of him,' said Melanie, 'and of you for figuring it out.' She tossed the loose end to Friday.

It was still a challenging climb, but with all the added upper body strength from so many burpees half-walking and half-pulling herself up, Friday was soon at the top.

'So, do you know who did it?' asked Melanie as Friday caught her breath.

'No,' said Friday, 'but I know how we can figure it out.'

Chapter 17

Heartbeat

Twenty minutes later, Friday and Melanie had met up with the Headmaster and taken him down to the PE staff room. Mr Fontana wasn't there when they arrived.

The PE staff room was organised but cluttered. Cricket bats rested against the wall, waiting to have their handles replaced or their timber oiled, various pads were stacked on a chair for their velcro to be mended, and piles of paperwork for various sporting schedules and transport arrangements lay littered across Mr Fontana's desk. The room smelled faintly of sweat and ageing leather.

'The art vandal has struck again,' observed Friday.

'What?' said the Headmaster.

Friday pointed to the poster on the wall. It showed Jesse Owens launching into a sprint at the 1936 Berlin Olympics.

'What about it?' asked the Headmaster.

'I'm pretty sure that Jesse Owens didn't have a mobile phone,' said Friday.

The Headmaster looked closer. There was definitely a smartphone in Jesse Owens' hand. In his runner's pose, it even looked as if he was holding the phone to his ear.

'Is that why you've dragged me down here?' demanded the Headmaster. 'You know I prefer to have as little to do with the physical education program as possible.'

'Don't we all,' observed Melanie.

'I know how we can find out who's been cutting holes in the perimeter fence,' said Friday.

'Does it have something to do with sport, then?' asked the Headmaster.

'In a way, yes,' said Friday. 'Or, rather, sport at an unusual time.'

The Headmaster rolled his eyes. 'Please don't talk in riddles. Just explain what's going on.'

'We know that the hole was cut in the fence between 7 pm at night and 7 am the following morning,' said Friday.

'Yes,' agreed the Headmaster. 'So?'

'Well, it's starting to get dark at 7 pm,' said Friday. 'Dinner is served at 6 pm. So, at 7 o'clock, most students are winding down: finishing off assignments, reading, getting ready for bed.'

'Clearly not our culprit,' said the Headmaster.

'Exactly,' said Friday. 'Not only are they going for a walk – then cutting through a fence, which would be strenuous enough – they are going for a long and difficult bike ride in the dark.'

'What's your point?' demanded the Headmaster.

'Their heart rate would be peaking,' said Friday. 'And it would be at a sustained peak for a long time.'

'Oh, I know where you're going,' said Melanie.

'I don't,' said the Headmaster. 'Explain yourself.'

'All the students are wearing fitness trackers,' said Friday, holding up her wrist.

'You're not,' said the Headmaster.

'No, I'm not,' agreed Friday, realising how silly the gesture was. 'But I'm the only one – well, me and Epstein.'

'He smashed his with a brick when he thought no one was looking,' explained Melanie.

'Why?' asked the Headmaster.

'He's a teenage boy,' said Friday. 'It's part of every boy's journey to manhood to act out in rebellion against a father figure in some way. You know, the classic Oedipal thing.'

'I wish I hadn't asked,' said the Headmaster.

'All the other students are wearing trackers,' continued Friday. 'They measure steps taken, staircases climbed and heart rate. Which means all we have to do is check the data and see which student had a heart rate at a sustained high for forty minutes last night.'

'Those trackers can really tell you that?' asked the Headmaster.

'Yes,' said Friday. 'All the information is collected here, on Mr Fontana's computer.'

'That's brilliant,' said the Headmaster. 'If I'd known the technology was available, I'd have installed the students with trackers years ago. Show me the data.'

Friday went over and sat down by the computer. It was on, but it was password-protected.

'We'll have to wait for Mr Fontana in order to get his password,' said the Headmaster.

'Or we could guess it,' said Friday. 'All we have to do is get into Mr Fontana's mind and think as he would think so we can imagine what password he would choose.'

'Try "burpee",' said Melanie. 'He loves those.'

Friday typed in 'burpee' but it failed.

'Tigers,' suggested the Headmaster. 'That's his favourite football team.'

Friday typed in 'tigers' but again access was denied, and this time a warning message came up saying she would get just one more attempt before she was locked out.

'Star jump?' suggested Melanie.

'Fitness?' suggested the Headmaster.

'I don't think we're on the right track,' said Friday. 'We're not really tapping into Mr Fontana's mentality. He's simpler than that.'

'How much simpler can you get than "star jump"?' asked Melanie.

'Statistically, the most commonly used password,' said Friday, 'is "password".'

'But that's just stupid,' said the Headmaster.

'Then that could be it,' said Melanie.

Friday typed in 'password'. There was a pause as the computer processed the command, then the home screen flicked up. The fitness tracker program was in the top right corner of the desktop. Friday double-clicked on the icon.

A large spreadsheet opened up. There were 350 students at the school, which meant there was a lot of data. But it was all conveniently collated in graph form. Friday clicked on the 'Heart Rate' icon, then selected the data from Tuesday. She scrolled across to 8 pm on the horizontal axis. Now it was just a question of scrolling through the long list of students. As Friday had surmised, almost the entire student body had a very low heart rate at that time. Melanie's was the lowest of all.

'Did you slip into a coma?' asked Friday, impressed that her friend could still function with such low blood pressure.

'I don't think so,' said Melanie. 'But sometimes it's hard for even me to tell.'

As she continued to scroll through, Friday noted that Binky had an elevated heart rate for twenty minutes.

'He's working on his squats,' said Melanie. 'I'm not sure what that means. But I think it's got something to do with going to the weights room and lifting heavy things every night to make himself stronger.'

'That fits,' said Friday, 'because his heart rate is elevated but he hasn't taken many steps. You'd need at least seven hundred steps to get from the school to the perimeter fence.'

'Keep scrolling down,' said the Headmaster.

'We're almost through all the students,' said Friday. 'The list started with year 7 and now I'm down to year 12.'

'What on earth do you think you are doing?!' yelled Mr Fontana.

The Headmaster stood up. He had been bending over alongside Friday to look at the screen, so Mr Fontana had not been able to see him from the doorway.

'Oh, sorry, sir, I didn't realise it was you,' said Mr Fontana.

'That's all right,' said the Headmaster. 'Sorry to disturb you. We just needed to access your data to deal with a disciplinary matter. Someone's been sneaking out of the school grounds. We're using the fitness tracker data to figure out who.'

'You are?' said Mr Fontana. He looked shocked. 'But isn't that a violation of student privacy?'

The Headmaster looked at Mr Fontana as if he had two heads. 'Students don't have privacy,' said the Headmaster. 'They only use privacy to get up to wickedness, and I won't have any of that.'

'I don't think this is appropriate,' said Mr Fontana. 'It's a breach of trust.'

'Oh, don't worry, Mr Fontana,' said Melanie. 'None of the students trust you.'

'Oh dear,' said Friday, her finger frozen over the computer mouse.

'What is it?' asked the Headmaster.

'We've found the culprit,' said Friday.

'We have?' asked the Headmaster. 'Who is it?' He checked his watch. 'The timing is perfect. I can call the parents and suspend the blighter and not be late for dinner.'

'I don't think it's going to be as easy as that,' said Friday, as she swung around in the swivel chair to face Mr Fontana. 'Because the only person with an

elevated heart rate at that time was not a student —
it was Mr Fontana.'

Mr Fontana looked startled. He glanced at the
fitness tracker on his wrist, and covered it with his
other hand as if that would somehow hide his guilt.

'What?' asked the Headmaster.

'It makes sense,' said Friday. 'Only someone
superbly fit would think that zip-lining off an escarpment and mountain-bike riding in the dark through a
forest would be an efficient way of getting from A to B.'

Mr Fontana smiled a little. Even though he had
been caught out, he always did enjoy it when people
noticed that he was superbly fit.

'And Mr Fontana would have access to heavy
duty metal-cutting machines,' said Friday, 'because
on weekends he is a volunteer firefighter.'

'How did you know that?' asked Mr Fontana.

'You flick light switches on with the back of your
knuckles,' said Friday. 'That's something firefighters
are taught to do, to avoid electrocution in water-
soaked buildings.'

'But where was he going?' asked the Headmaster.

'And why was he wearing ladies' shoes?' asked
Melanie.

'I was not!' declared Mr Fontana.

'No,' said Friday, 'he was wearing smooth-soled shoes, the imprint looked like a lady's high heel. But men's shoes can look like that, too.'

'What sort of men's shoes?' asked the Headmaster. He had never worn anything other than the most boring brogues himself.

'A dancing shoe,' said Friday. 'It can't have been a tap shoe, or the plates would have left an imprint. So perhaps some sort of Latin dancing footwear. Salsa or tango?'

Mr Fontana hung his head in shame. 'They're for the tango.'

'You did all this to go tango dancing?' asked the Headmaster.

'I suspect there is more to it than that,' said Friday. 'That was a seriously nice mountain bike stashed out there in the forest. They can cost up to two or three thousand dollars. That's an expensive hobby – unless you have another hobby that you can use to pay for it.'

'What are you saying?' asked the Headmaster.

'I'm saying that Mr Fontana has been sneaking out of the school every Tuesday night to teach a tango-dancing class in Stratham,' said Friday.

'He's been moonlighting!' exclaimed Melanie. 'And literally by moonlight.'

'I'm so sorry,' said Mr Fontana. 'I did it for the extra cash. And also because I really do love to dance.'

'I thought you were a rugby man,' said the Headmaster.

'You can be both,' said Mr Fontana. 'Dance is very good for improving your football footwork.'

'But why did you sneak out and why did you cut holes in my very expensive fence?' demanded the Headmaster.

'What else could I do?' asked Mr Fontana.

'Get a bus into town like a normal person,' said the Headmaster.

'You mean, you'd let me teach a tango class in town?' asked Mr Fontana.

'This isn't a prisoner-of-war camp,' said the Headmaster. 'If you want to pursue a hobby in your own time, that's your personal business.'

'But I thought I wasn't allowed to take on a second job,' said Mr Fontana.

'It's just a harmless hobby job,' said the Headmaster. 'How much can you possibly earn?'

'$750 a night,' said Mr Fontana. 'More for private workshops.'

'What?!' demanded the Headmaster.

'I'm very good at the tango,' explained Mr Fontana. 'People travel a long way for my lessons.'

'Then why on earth are you teaching here?' asked the Headmaster. 'I'd quit in a second if I could earn that kind of money.'

'I love teaching,' said Mr Fontana.

The Headmaster sighed. He patted Mr Fontana on the shoulder. 'Poor naïve fool. Good for you. You keep teaching the tango in the evenings. You have my blessing – on one condition.'

'What is it?' asked Mr Fontana.

'Please walk out the front gate,' said the Headmaster. 'No more damage to the steel fencing.'

Mr Fontana smiled. 'Thank you, sir.' He shook hands with the Headmaster.

'Not at all,' said the Headmaster. 'I'm happy for you that your hobby is so lucrative. It means you'll be able to afford to pay for the fence repairs in full so that the school council won't have to be notified.'

Chapter 18

The Great Unveiling

It was the morning of the art show. The scaffolding had been taken down during the night and replaced with giant sheets of cloth so that Mr Brecht's giant mural could be unveiled in front of a full crowd of parents, dignitaries and guests before they went in to start the bidding.

The Headmaster had a spring in his step for once. Normally he wasn't seen much about the school grounds. He preferred to hide in his office, eating chocolate biscuits and making decisions in splendid isolation. But for once things were going well, so the Headmaster sauntered about the school enjoying himself by reprimanding students for their untidy clothes and surprising staff by turning up in the doorway of their classrooms and telling them to 'just ignore me', knowing full well that was entirely impossible.

'Ah, Barnes,' said the Headmaster as he spotted Friday walking between classes. 'I want a word with you.'

'But I haven't done anything,' protested Friday.

'Exactly,' said the Headmaster, 'and I want it to stay that way. I don't suppose I could persuade you to go into town and watch a double feature or something? I'd buy the tickets and give you extra money for popcorn.'

'But if something goes wrong at the art show,' said Friday, 'wouldn't you want me there to help sort it out?'

'I know that logically makes sense,' said the Headmaster, 'but I can't help feeling that trouble is magnetically attracted to you.'

'That's impossible,' said Friday. 'Magneticism is generated by electric currents and magnetic moments of elementary particles. It's impossible for a person to be magnetic. Most documented cases of alleged "human magnets" actually turned out to be people who simply had sticky skin.'

'Yes, I'm sure according to the laws of physics it's impossible,' said the Headmaster, 'and yet according to the laws of probability it always seems to happen. Just behave.'

The Headmaster strode off, leaving Friday feeling unfairly maligned.

At 5 o'clock that afternoon the guests started to arrive. A lot of parents were turning up. Very few of them had ever thought their children had any artistic ability, so they were curious to see if being taught by the great Lysander Brecht had any effect. The Headmaster had also invited everyone from the local community. A few free finger sandwiches and some champagne would go a long way to smoothing the ruffled feathers of their neighbours. And feathers did get very ruffled during the course of an academic year. Local residents did not enjoy the constant traffic of runaway students trying to get out, and domestic staff smuggling contraband in. So there was a large crowd milling around in the quadrangle, drinks in hand, waiting for the great unveiling.

'If I could have your attention, please,' said the Headmaster, standing at the podium at the base of the flagpole. 'Thank you so much for coming to our event tonight. We at Highcrest Academy have been so honoured to have Lysander Brecht join us for the last eight weeks. I'm sure he has been an inspirational teacher, and our students will remember the experience of working with him for the rest of their lives.'

'I'm sure Travis will remember eating his brie,' whispered Melanie.

'Mr Brecht, come up here,' said the Headmaster.

Friday looked across to see Mr Brecht scowl. The crowd applauded. He reluctantly climbed the few steps to where the Headmaster was standing.

'Thank you, Mr Brecht, for sharing your talent with us,' said the Headmaster, 'for teaching the students, for arranging this art show and for designing the grand mural, which we are about to unveil. Perhaps you could say a few words.'

The Headmaster stepped back to allow Mr Brecht his turn at the microphone. Mr Brecht glared at the Headmaster, then turned and glared at the whole crowd. 'No, I don't want to make a speech,' said Mr Brecht. 'It's bad enough I've had to teach the children; I won't be a performing monkey for their parents as well.'

The Headmaster hastily stepped between Mr Brecht and the microphone. 'Yes, thank you. Such an insight into the artistic mind,' said the Headmaster. 'Well, with no further ado, I call upon the vice president of the school council, Dame Lynley Hasbeth, to do the honours and unveil our mural, designed by Lysander Brecht and completed by every single member of our student body. Dame Lynley . . .'

A thin, elderly woman in a beautiful grey silk dress and wearing diamond jewellery stepped forward, hung her clutch purse from her elbow and reached up to pull the cord controlling the curtain. The curtain didn't move.

'It's stuck,' said Dame Lynley.

'Perhaps, Dame Lynley,' said the Headmaster, beginning to look a little flustered, 'perhaps if you pull harder?'

Dame Lynley reached up and yanked as hard as an elderly woman who doesn't weigh much more than a dish rag could. The curtain swayed slightly but didn't open.

'Binky!' snapped the Headmaster.

'Yes, sir,' said Binky. Being six foot five, he was easy to spot in the crowd.

'Help Dame Lynley,' ordered the Headmaster.

'Yes, sir,' said Binky. He jogged over to Dame Lynley. 'Shall we pull it together, Your Highness?'

Dame Lynley, enjoying being spoken to by a very handsome athletic boy, grabbed the cord again. Binky reached up as high as he could and, using the strength of every muscle in his large body, wrenched the cord down. Dame Lynley, who had been standing too close, was knocked over by his bottom as he dropped into a squat. Binky, trying desperately hard not to step on an elderly woman he mistakenly believed was a member of the royal family, tripped over her and fell hard on his back. The curtain juddered for a moment, then completely fell away. And in that instant everyone totally forgot about the elderly woman who Binky may very well have crushed, as they stared at the profoundly confronting sight of the mural.

'Good gracious!' exclaimed the Headmaster. 'What have you done?!'

Mr Brecht burst out laughing. 'Fabulous, isn't she?'

The mural was a six metre by thirty metre painting of Mrs Cannon, entirely naked and reading a book. Her modesty was only protected by the discreet placement of the book and a coffee cup.

'But that's Mrs Cannon!' exploded the Headmaster.

'I look rather good, don't I?' said Mrs Cannon happily.

'She's completely naked!' exclaimed the Headmaster.

'I call it, "The Importance of Literacy",' said Mr Brecht.

'It's a nude painting of the English teacher!' yelled the Headmaster.

'What better way to encourage young boys to read,' said Mr Brecht.

'They're not going to read!' yelled the Headmaster. 'They're going to be too busy staring at the naked painting!'

'Yes,' agreed Mr Brecht, 'I am here to teach art appreciation.'

'It's not the art they'll be appreciating!' bellowed the Headmaster.

'I like to think that Mrs Cannon raises teaching to an art form,' said Mr Brecht.

'So gallant,' said Mrs Cannon, smiling at Mr Brecht.

'And what is Mr Cannon going to think about all this?' demanded the Headmaster, turning on Mrs Cannon. 'Do you think he's going to be happy about having a two-hundred-square-metre painting of his wife naked?'

'Of course he is,' said Mrs Cannon. 'Who do you think took the photograph it was based on?'

The Headmaster clutched his head in frustration. 'I shouldn't be trying to improve morale at this school, I should be trying to improve mental health. You're all bonkers!'

'Your school has the world's largest Lysander Brecht painting,' said Friday, calling out from the front of the crowd. 'It's going to look impressive in the school prospectus.'

'I can't put a picture of Mrs Cannon in her birthday suit in the prospectus!' wailed the Headmaster.

'I'd be keen to see a copy if you did,' said one billionaire.

'Come along,' said Mr Brecht, looking at his watch. 'It's time to start the art show. The international bidders will be waiting on the phones.'

'I want to fire you,' said the Headmaster.

'My contract expires at midnight,' said Mr Brecht. 'You'd only be creating a lot of paperwork for yourself. Come on, let's see if we can raise enough money for your pool.'

Chapter 19

▰▱▰▱▰▱▰▱▰▱▰▱▰

The Art Show

When Friday walked into the school hall she did not expect to be impressed, but she was. Mr Brecht's overblown budget had obviously extended to art show decorations as well. The whole room, which was the size of a basketball court plus bleachers, had been swathed in white sheeting. Partitions had been set up at carefully arranged 'random' angles to display the work.

Objectively, as she glanced about the room,

Friday had to concede that the art works were rather good. Highcrest Academy wasn't renowned for its arts program, and she had certainly seen no evidence of artistic excellence from the student body before, but Mr Brecht's visceral teaching style seemed to have had an effect. As a whole, the student body of Highcrest was marginally less terrible than they had been before Mr Brecht arrived.

The parents and guests were in high spirits, having been titillated by the enormous nude painting spread across the school's main classroom block. Champagne was being handed around. There was a frisson of excitement in the air.

Mr Hambling, the drama teacher, stepped forward to take the microphone. Mr Hambling was a former Shakespearean actor who had trodden the boards at Stratford-Upon-Avon and Broadway. Admittedly, he had never made it much beyond playing Spear Holder Number Two or Third Soothsayer from the Left, but in his time in the theatre he had learned to speak very loudly and dramatically. There really was no need to amplify the sound of his voice, but he enjoyed using a microphone as it allowed him even greater range for being melodramatic.

'Ladies and gentlemen, honoured guests and students, we are gathered here today for one purpose,' declared Mr Hambling. He looked about the room, making sure he had everyone's attention. 'To make a vast amount of money for this school!'

Everyone clapped and cheered. They really were in a good mood, the champagne apparently having disconnected the part of their brains that made them realise they were the ones who were going to be separated from this vast amount of money.

'We are going to auction off the three finest paintings from each year,' said Mr Hambling. 'We will begin with year 7. The first item for sale today is a watercolour by Jessica Bastionne titled "Swamp Frog".'

Binky stepped forward with the picture and placed it on an easel next to Mr Hambling. It was actually a lovely painting. The frog looked almost majestic as it sat proudly on a rock, glistening in the sun, its jowls swollen like a proud leader. Friday pondered that she could see how the fairytales of frogs turning into princes had originated. For a slimy, mud-dwelling amphibian, this frog looked like it had a tremendous sense of self-importance.

'Who will start the bidding?' asked Mr Hambling.

Everyone turned to look at Mr and Mrs Bastionne, Jessica's parents. If there was any parent who might feel uninclined to give more money to the school, Mr and Mrs Bastionne would be prime candidates. Just the previous term Jessica had been violently ill after eating contaminated beef stroganoff. The Headmaster had only managed to avoid a lawsuit against the school by promising to 'review' Jessica's history mark, which basically meant he had allowed her to pass modern history even though she had studied the subject for a while and still misspelled 'Hitler' as 'Hilter'.

'Who will start me off with a bid for this fine watercolour of a wide-mouthed brown frog?' asked Mr Hambling. 'It would be a delight to display in any home. In the lavatory, perhaps.'

Mr Bastionne put his hand up. '$50,' he said proudly. Jessica squealed and clapped, and rushed over to kiss her father on the cheek.

'$50 for the frog, do I have any other bids?' asked Mr Hambling. 'Will anybody give me sixty? Going once . . . going twice . . . going . . .'

'$100!'

Everyone spun around. At the back of the hall was a trestle table with five old-fashioned, corded telephones set out in a row. A member of the teaching staff was manning each phone. Mr Davies had the handset to his ear. He held a paddle in his hand and called out again. '$100!'

'Are they taking phone bids?' Friday whispered to Melanie.

'Of course, so many of the parents are overseas,' said Melanie.

'On holidays?' asked Friday.

'Some, yes,' said Melanie, 'but a lot are just tax exiles.'

'But who other than Jessica's own parents would want to buy her painting?' asked Friday.

'One of her grandparents, perhaps,' suggested Melanie. 'Or someone who really likes frogs.'

'$100,' said Mr Hambling, enjoying the drama of the situation. 'Do I hear two hundred?' He looked meaningfully at Mr Bastionne.

Mr Bastionne scowled. His wife tapped him hard on the arm. He begrudgingly held his paddle aloft and called out, '$150.'

Mr Hambling smiled and was about to call for

any more bids when Mr Davies again called out from the back of the room. '$500.'

There was a gasp of astonishment from the crowd. It was a good painting of a frog, but it wasn't *that* good.

'Wow,' said Melanie. 'My grandfather is a billionaire, but I don't think even he would pay $500 for a picture I did.'

'$500,' said Mr Hambling. 'Do I have any further bids?'

Everyone looked at Mr Bastionne. Even his wife scowled now. Mr Bastionne turned to Jessica. 'Would you forgive me if I didn't buy your painting?'

'No,' said Jessica.

'What if I paid you $250 to forgive me?' asked Mr Bastionne.

'Oh, Daddy!' exclaimed Jessica. 'I love you so much.'

Mr Bastionne took out his wallet and started counting cash out to his daughter.

Mr Hambling picked up his gavel and slammed it on the rostrum. 'Sold to the telephone bidder for $500.'

Binky removed the painting and brought over the next item.

'Next, we have a painting by one of our high-profile students, Ian Wainscott,' said Mr Hambling.

The painting was put on the easel and revealed. It was a large canvas depicting a vase full of flowers, but it was the angriest representation of flowers that Friday had ever seen.

'How does he get a jug full of flowers to look so cross?' asked Melanie.

'I think the liberal use of red and the violently abrupt brushstrokes have most of the effect,' said Friday.

'If you squint at it, the dahlias on the left look like his father's face,' said Melanie.

'Who will start the bidding for this . . . provocative work?' asked Mr Hambling.

Everyone looked about. Ian's parents weren't there.

'His father must still be in the Cayman Islands,' said Melanie.

'He could be living in a house across the street and he still wouldn't bother to come,' said Friday.

Suddenly the back door of the hall burst open. A large, scruffy man wearing a crumpled hat stumbled into the hall, bumping into the trestle table with phones.

'Uncle Bernie!' exclaimed Friday.

'Is that Ian Wainscott's picture?' asked Uncle Bernie.

'Yes, it is,' said Mr Hambling, who was enjoying himself. They were only up to the second item in the auction, and this evening was already proving to be more dramatic than the bloodiest rendition of *Macbeth*.

'I bid $100!' called Uncle Bernie.

Everyone clapped. There wasn't a person in the room who would have taken the painting unless they had been paid $100 and been allowed to hang it facing the wall.

'Do I have any other bids?' asked Mr Hambling.

Everyone looked at the phone bank. Mr Davies shook his head.

'Sold to the scruffy man in the grey fedora,' said Mr Hambling.

Uncle Bernie spotted Friday in the crowd and went over to join her and Melanie.

'That was very kind of you, Uncle Bernie,' said Friday. 'Unless you like abstract impressionist art on the theme of anger, then your motives would be purely selfish.'

'Helena is away on a permaculture workshop,' said Uncle Bernie, 'and when I realised Ian had a piece in the auction I couldn't let it go unbid for.'

'You're not my father.'

They turned to see Ian standing right behind Uncle Bernie. His fists were clenched like he wanted to hit him. But that would have been silly. Uncle Bernie was six foot two, so only a couple of inches taller than Ian, but he was almost as wide as he was tall, and even though there was a lot of fat on him there was a lot of muscle under the fat, which was left over from his days as a former professional ice-hockey player.

'I know,' said Uncle Bernie.

'It's not for you to buy my painting,' said Ian.

'Your mum would want me to,' said Uncle Bernie.

'Really?' said Ian. 'Did she even know about this art show?'

'I don't know what she did or didn't know,' said Uncle Bernie. 'She's at a retreat where they don't have phone service.'

'Did she ever mention the art show to you, or that she wanted you to buy my painting?' asked Ian.

'Not as such,' said Uncle Bernie. 'But it is spring. There's a lot going on in her garden right now.'

'Typical,' spat out Ian. He turned and stormed away.

'It's so unfair that boys aren't allowed to cry publicly,' said Melanie. 'I really do think it would do him good to have a sob.'

'But it wouldn't do his image any good,' said Friday. 'And I think he's more concerned with his image than his mental health.'

'The next item in our catalogue is a beauty,' said Mr Hambling. 'It would look lovely on the wall of your living room or your dining room, hanging over you as you eat.'

Binky brought the next painting over to the easel.

'It's by our very own in-house busybody, Friday Barnes,' said Mr Hambling.

The crowd muttered. Friday had developed quite a reputation. She had been responsible for either getting many of the students out of trouble or into trouble, so the parents knew exactly who she was.

Binky unveiled the painting. It was a large oil painting of a football match.

'You painted football?' asked Melanie.

'This work is called "Exercise in Futility",' continued Mr Hambling.

'I find football poignant in its pointless, exhausting brutality,' said Friday.

'It's a really pretty picture,' said Uncle Bernie. 'You've captured a beautiful scene: the late afternoon sun and the rolling expanse of the school grounds. It's lovely.'

'Yes,' said Friday. 'I'm still not very good at the expressive elements of art. I can depict what something looks like, but I struggle to get the sense of contempt I have for it into my work.'

'Who will start the bidding?' asked Mr Hambling.

'$100,' said Uncle Bernie.

'Thanks, Uncle Bernie,' said Friday, 'but you don't have to. I know how much insurance investigators earn. And you did just buy Ian's painting.'

'I can afford another hundred dollars,' said Uncle Bernie.

'One hundred and fifty!'

They turned to see Mr Fontana holding up his paddle. He smiled at Friday. 'You can't play sport, Barnes, but that's a great picture of my team playing rugby.'

Uncle Bernie swallowed hard. He looked down at his own paddle. Friday took hold of his hand. 'Don't do it,' said Friday. 'I'll paint you anything you want for free.'

'You really won't mind?' asked Uncle Bernie.

'If you paid hundreds of dollars for that,' said Friday, 'I'd be upset worrying how you're going to afford to pay for all the home-delivered pizza you must secretly order when Mrs Wainscott goes to sleep at night.'

'How did you know?' asked Uncle Bernie.

'Because I know you,' said Friday. 'And because you have a perfectly round stain the exact size and colour of a slice of pepperoni on your shirt.'

'$200!'

Everyone turned. It was Mr Davies with a phone bidder again.

Mr Fontana defiantly held up his paddle again. '$300,' he declared.

'Do we have a further bid from our phone bidder?' asked Mr Hambling.

Mr Davies was listening on the phone. He had a look of confusion on his face. 'Are you sure?' he was heard to say. Even though he was speaking softly, everyone could hear because the room had fallen silent. Mr Davies looked up. '$5000.'

Everyone burst into applause.

'How generous!' exclaimed Mr Hambling. 'Someone must really want Highcrest Academy to have its own pool.'

'$6000!' called Mr Fontana.

'What's he doing!' exclaimed Friday.

'He can afford it with all those high-priced tango lessons,' said Melanie.

Everyone was looking at Mr Davies on the telephone again. He was nodding as he listened. He looked up and called out, '$20,000!'

Everyone was stunned.

'Mr Fontana, any further bids?' asked Mr Hambling.

Mr Fontana shook his head.

'Sold to the bidder on the telephone!' declared Mr Hambling as he cracked his gavel on the lectern.

'I don't believe it,' said Friday.

'I always thought you'd end up having a career in law enforcement,' said Uncle Bernie. 'But if you're that talented, maybe you should consider becoming an artist instead.'

'No way!' said Friday. 'I don't care how good I am at painting. I like puzzles. I know some people enjoy creative expression, but I don't get it at all.'

And so, as the evening continued, many paintings went for what you would expect – one or two hundred dollars, paid for by a relative. Maybe five hundred, if the relative was showing off. But about a quarter of the paintings went for exorbitant prices and all to telephone bidders.

'What do you think is going on?' asked Friday.

'Maybe it's the overseas parents feeling really guilty about not being here,' said Melanie.

'Maybe it's a money laundering scheme,' suggested Uncle Bernie. 'That's usually what's going on when people are overpaying tens of thousands of dollars for something.'

'But it's hard to launder money through a school's books,' said Friday.

'Unless you're the Headmaster,' said Melanie.

'If the Headmaster had extra money, he would launder it through his bookie,' said Friday.

'Maybe it's a construction scam,' said Uncle Bernie. 'The company building the pool could be in on it.'

The Headmaster took the stage. 'Thank you all very much for coming, especially the parents who bid on paintings. Your generosity is very much appreciated. The students at Highcrest have long enjoyed the finest quality polo pitches, cricket grounds and classrooms – it's good to know that they will soon enjoy a state-of-the-art heated indoor swimming pool as well.'

Everyone applauded, partly with enthusiasm and partly to hurry the Headmaster up.

'If you won the bidding on an item, please step forward,' said the Headmaster. 'Miss Priddock will take your payment – cash or credit card will be accepted – then you can take your painting home. The paintings won by phone bidders will be packaged up and shipped to their addresses first thing in the morning.'

'Stop!' yelled Friday.

The Headmaster groaned. 'Urgh, I knew this was going too well. Heaven forbid we have a school occasion where Miss Barnes doesn't interrupt and turn everything on its head.'

'I cannot allow this to continue,' declared Friday as she pushed her way to the front of the crowd.

'What?' said the Headmaster. 'You can't allow the school to hold a successful fundraiser?'

'No,' said Friday, 'I can't allow large-scale fraud to take place.'

Chapter 20

The Truth Revealed

Now the crowd was muttering excitedly. This was proving to be the most entertaining school function of all time. The massive nude mural had been wonderful. The champagne was a nice touch. Now the promise of a huge scandal had everyone energised.

'We should be charging people $50 a head for tonight's dramatic entertainment,' said Mr Hambling.

'I know,' agreed Mrs Cannon. 'In just two hours

we've had way more action than an entire Jane Austen novel.'

Friday had made her way up onto the stage.

'Would you like the microphone, Barnes?' asked the Headmaster sarcastically.

But Friday was terrible at picking sarcasm.

'Yes, that's probably a good idea,' said Friday. 'It will save me having to yell.' She took the microphone from the Headmaster's hand and turned to face the audience. 'No one will be taking home any of these paintings tonight.'

'But I just paid $200 for my son's awful painting of a rosebush,' complained Mr Patel.

'Dad,' moaned Patel, clearly embarrassed.

'You can't take them home,' said Friday, 'because they are all evidence.'

'Of what?' asked the Headmaster. 'Large-scale art appreciation?'

'No. What has happened here tonight has been an elaborate charade to commit massive tax fraud,' said Friday.

'Have you been sniffing the craft glue, Barnes?' said Mr Brecht. 'I've never heard of anything so ridiculous in my life.'

'How else do you explain these ludicrous prices?' asked Friday.

'Hasn't it occurred to you that I am the country's most famous artist?' said Mr Brecht. 'This event has been publicised globally on the internet and in established art community periodicals. These bidders are paying a premium for the paintings because they want a painting by one of my students.'

'Perhaps,' said Friday, 'but I don't think so. Binky, could you please fetch my painting of the football match?'

Binky found Friday's painting and put it up on the easel.

'I think it is much more likely,' continued Friday, 'that the bidders have paid a premium for these paintings because of what's underneath.'

Friday reached over to the painting and started picking at the corner of the paint.

'What are you doing!' exclaimed the Headmaster. 'Someone's paid good money for that!'

Mr Brecht lunged forward and grabbed Friday by the arms. 'Stop it!' he bellowed.

'Let her go!' hollered Uncle Bernie. People leapt out of his way as he started storming towards the stage.

'Binky!' cried Friday. 'Peel off the paint, now!'

Binky was not the most agile thinker, but he was excellent at doing as he was told. And Binky had a lot of respect for Friday. He held her in even higher regard than the Headmaster, although not quite as high as his regard for the rugby coach. He saw the corner of paint that Friday had peeled up and he pulled.

Friday's entire painting of a football match started to pull away like a rectangular banana peel. Everyone fell silent when they saw what was underneath. A savagely powerful expressionist painting of a pigeon.

'Behold!' declared Friday. 'An original Lysander Brecht!'

'What's the meaning of this?' asked the Headmaster.

'Mr Brecht is in far greater financial trouble than you may have realised,' said Friday.

'I knew he had tax debt,' said the Headmaster. 'That's why he took a teaching job.'

'Yes, but people in tax debt often owe money to other people as well,' said Friday. 'Like the bank that gave him a car loan. They repossessed his red sports car, but only after he used it to swindle Mr Maclean out of $10,000.'

'Why is this the first I'm hearing about this?' asked the Headmaster.

'Then there was the kidnapping attempt,' continued Friday.

'But that was Marcus Welby,' said the Headmaster.

'Yes,' agreed Friday, 'but the two fake police officers came to this school asking to see a tall, thin, red-haired fourteen-year-old boy. It was actually you who matched the description to Marcus Welby. But that description would also match Epstein Smythe.'

'It does?' asked the Headmaster.

'It might surprise you to know,' said Friday, 'that black with blue tips is not Epstein's natural hair colour.'

This obviously hadn't occurred to the Headmaster because he now looked at Epstein's head, clearly very puzzled.

'The men had been spying on the school for some time. They'd been seen in the woods by the golf course and watching with binoculars,' said Friday. 'Ian thought they were criminal connections of his father, but in fact they were looking for Epstein.'

'But why would anyone want to kidnap Epstein Smythe?' asked the Headmaster.

'Because he is Mr Brecht's son,' said Friday.

'Now, Friday . . .' blustered the Headmaster.

'There's no point denying it,' said Friday. 'There is too much evidence to support my assertion. Mr Brecht and Epstein arrived on the same day. No doubt Epstein's tuition was part of Mr Brecht's payment package. They are both tall, attractive red-heads. Although Mr Brecht's faded auburn hair is more white than red these days. Epstein claims he loathes art, a typical teenage rebellion against his father.'

'I didn't want to pander to his ego,' said Epstein angrily.

'And yet you have inherited your father's great artistic talent,' said Friday. 'Which is why you were able to perfectly graffiti so many pictures around the school. That was you, wasn't it? You vandalised "The Red Princess" because the red-haired baby is a portrait of you. You didn't want anyone to notice the resemblance and tease you. Then, like so many criminals, you developed a taste for the crime. You kept graffitiing more and more pictures. But it did mean that you had to smash your fitness tracker so no one could follow your movements.'

Epstein nodded.

'It makes sense,' said Friday. 'The only other person talented enough to do it is your father, and he's too preoccupied with eating cheese, dating Miss Priddock and avoiding debt collectors to indulge in such an intricate practical joke.'

'Debt collectors?!' exclaimed the Headmaster. 'I thought his pay cheque to teach here was going to cover that.'

'Mr Brecht owes money to the tax department and his car loan provider. It would not be surprising that he owes money to even more unsavoury types who resort to kidnapping children to get their money back,' said Friday. 'Which is why he has been using the art auction as an opportunity to smuggle his paintings out of the country,' said Friday. 'So that he won't have to declare the income he earns to the tax department.'

Mr Brecht let Friday go and backed away. 'You're not going to believe her, are you?' said Mr Brecht. 'It's a crazy accusation.'

'Normally I would agree with you,' said the Headmaster. 'But over the past year I have learned that Miss Barnes's crazy accusations are almost always true.'

'And how else do you explain the painting under the painting?' asked Friday. 'You told us you primed the canvases yourself. It would have been easy for you to use a special acrylic paint that would protect your own painting but peel off easily when it arrives at the bidder.'

'My paintings are worth far more than the mere thousands that have been bid here tonight,' said Mr Brecht.

'That's because all they are paying for tonight is just the packaging and handling,' said Friday. 'The real payment for your pictures would have been transferred to your bank account in some tax haven, like the Cayman Islands.'

'You can't prove anything,' said Mr Brecht.

'I think she already has,' said Sergeant Crowley as he mounted the steps towards the stage. He picked up Jessica Bastionne's picture of a frog and pulled at the corner of the painting. He soon had the whole picture peeling away to reveal a landscape of a beached whale. 'The paintings are here. An art analyst will be able to confirm that these are yours, and in this day and age of computer technology it's never been easier to send money overseas, but it's also never been easier for police to electronically trace the movement of money overseas.'

'What are you saying?' asked Mr Brecht.

'I'm saying that I am arresting you for –'

Sergeant Crowley never got to finish his sentence. Mr Brecht grabbed the Headmaster, shoved him hard at the sergeant, knocking both men over, and started to run. He leapt off the stage and was out the door in a millisecond. But Friday was quick on his heels.

Friday had never been athletic, but weeks and weeks of burpees every morning had had an effect. She actually managed to keep up with Mr Brecht as he ran out to the school parking lot. He yanked open the door of his old station wagon and only just shut the door in time as Friday caught up with him and started pounding on the window.

'Mr Brecht, come back!' yelled Friday. 'You'll never get away with this!'

Mr Brecht ground the gears of his car, trying to find reverse, when suddenly his car lurched backwards. Friday jumped back in time before he could run over her toes. But Mr Brecht did not get far. Unfortunately, as was characteristic of the parents at Highcrest, a lot of them had parked very selfishly.

They were a self-important group at the best of times, but when hurrying to get to a school event that they didn't really want to attend, none of them thought that the unsaid rules of a parking lot and common courtesy applied to them. They had parked each other in terribly. So as Mr Brecht hurried to get away, there wasn't enough room for him to back up properly, and he slammed into a brand new Mercedes SUV.

Everyone winced. By this time, the whole gathering had left the school hall and congregated outside to witness the spectacle.

Mr Brecht threw the car into gear and accelerated forward. But there was a Porsche in the way, and he scraped all along an entire side of its paintwork as he tried to turn towards the entrance. He finally got his car away from the Porsche only to rear-end a BMW. In the next two minutes Mr Brecht managed to scrape, bang into or outright smash up a Lamborghini, two Volvos, an antique Jaguar, three Audis and a Toyota Corolla before he finally gave up, threw open the door of his car and set off running.

Friday chased after him. 'Stop!' she called.

But Mr Brecht ran faster. The school gates were a good eight hundred metres from the front of the school building, and eight hundred metres is a long way when you're trying to run at full pace. Especially if you are an artist too sophisticated to engage in exercise, and whose arteries are clogged due to eating an inordinate amount of cheese. Mr Brecht was soon coughing and gasping for breath. Friday was gaining on him. By the time he reached the school gates, Friday was close on his heels. He leapt up to start climbing over, and Friday slammed into the fence and grabbed his foot.

'Let go!' yelled Mr Brecht.

'No!' yelled Friday, clinging to his foot even tighter. But then her grip slipped as Mr Brecht's shoe came off in her hand.

Mr Brecht pulled himself up higher onto the fence. Friday wasn't giving up. She leapt up and grabbed his other foot.

'Let go!' Mr Brecht yelled again.

'You have to face up to your crimes,' said Friday through gritted teeth as she desperately clung to Mr Brecht's foot. Mr Brecht tightened his grip on the gate with his hands, lifted his free foot from the railing and stomped down on Friday's face. Friday's nose exploded in pain. Mr Brecht wrenched his foot out of her grasp and she fell back onto the gravel driveway, now clutching both of his shoes. Friday couldn't see much anymore because her eyes filled with tears, one of those inexplicable things the body does when it's struck in the nose. But she did make out a flurry of movement as someone leapt over her and grabbed Mr Brecht around the waist. Friday blinked several times.

It was Ian. He was now dangling from Mr Brecht's belt as Mr Brecht dangled from the gate. Suddenly Mr Brecht's grip gave out, and both of them came tumbling down right on top of Friday.

When Friday woke up, she was lying on the grass. She could see twinkling lights above her. At first she thought this was a symptom of concussion, then she realised she was literally seeing stars because it was night time and she was outside. She turned her head to see Mr Brecht. He was also lying down, but unlike Friday he was face down with his hands handcuffed behind his back.

'Are you okay?'

Friday turned the other way to see Ian crouching over her. She was about to say she was fine, but she temporarily forgot how to speak when she realised that Ian wasn't wearing a shirt. He was getting very muscly for a thirteen-year-old.

'Are you all right?' Ian asked again.

'Why aren't you wearing a shirt?' asked Friday. Friday's voice sounded nasal to her own ears, and she couldn't breathe through her nose at all.

'Because you're lying on it, nitwit,' said Ian. 'And you're supposed to be the hyper vigilant one.'

Friday's brain processed this information. She was lying on the ground but she wasn't wet. The ground should be dewy at this time of night, so obviously she was lying on something.

'Aren't you cold?' asked Friday.

'No, running down here to save you warmed me up,' said Ian.

'So is Mr Brecht being arrested?' asked Friday.

'Yes, apart from the art fraud it turns out he's been charging his outrageously expensive cheese to the school account,' said Ian. 'Plus, he did commit assault.'

'Who to?' asked Friday.

'You,' said Ian. 'Maybe it's more serious than we realised. Apart from the broken nose, perhaps you've got brain damage.'

'I've got a broken nose?!' Friday exclaimed. She reached up to touch her nose and immediately regretted it. The dull ache in her head instantly turned to a splintering sharp pain in her face.

'Ow,' said Friday weakly.

'Don't worry,' said Ian, 'Mr Fontana reset it for you while you were unconscious.'

'Mr Fontana?! Why not the nurse?' asked Friday.

'He runs quicker than the nurse,' explained Ian. 'He was the first one down here to help restrain Mr Brecht. Then when the nurse did get here she asked him to do it because he's the rugby master, so he's had loads more practice resetting noses than she has.'

'Does it look all right?' asked Friday.

'At the moment it looks purple and swollen like an eggplant,' said Ian.

Tears welled in Friday's eyes and she could not contain the first sob to bubble up inside her.

Ian looked more alarmed than he had facing a violent art criminal. 'Don't do that!' said Ian. 'It's fine. People break their noses all the time. You'll be able to breathe normally again in a day or two.'

'I don't want a broken nose,' said Friday, definitely weeping now. 'My face was plain enough to start with.'

Ian sighed. He sat down on the grass alongside Friday and put his hand on her shoulder. 'Your face is just fine.'

Friday blinked up at him through her tears. Ian wasn't smirking or rolling his eyes or doing any of the other telltale things he did when he was being sarcastic. Friday's chin trembled as she struggled to smile at him. Perhaps he really did think she looked fine.

Ian smiled back. His big, radiant, handsome smile. 'Besides, you can always grow your fringe really long so that no one can see your nose. Or perhaps get a bigger hat.' His eyes had their familiar cheeky look. He was teasing her now. Friday was too tired to think of anything clever to say in retort, so she weakly reached out and hit Ian instead. Which she immediately regretted because she found touching his bare chest very disconcerting.

'Here come the paramedics,' said Ian. 'Try

not to flirt with them the way you've been flirting with me.'

'What! I have not,' protested Friday.

'Yeah, yeah,' said Ian as he stood up to make way for the professionals.

Chapter 21

In Conclusion

The following morning, Friday gingerly made her way to the dining hall for breakfast. Everyone stared at her as she passed. She would like to think it was because her brilliant deductive reasoning had saved the school from yet another criminal conspiracy, but realistically she knew they were staring at the plastic splint over the bridge of her nose, which was held in place by two long strips of tape: one across her forehead and another from one cheekbone to the other.

'This is depressing,' said Friday. 'I feel bad because my face is a mess, and I feel bad for being so vain that I care how my face looks. It's lowering to realise I'm more superficial than I thought.'

'On the bright side,' said Melanie, 'it does distract everyone from your ugly cardigan.'

Friday looked down at the navy blue cardigan she was wearing. 'I'm not wearing my ugly cardigan, I'm wearing your nice blue one.'

'Oh yes. And yet, somehow you manage to wear it in such a way that it looks exactly the same on you,' said Melanie.

'I suppose you were right about one thing,' said Friday.

'I was?' said Melanie, pleasantly surprised.

'I did end up with three head injuries,' said Friday, pointing to her nose.

'So you did,' said Melanie. 'Hopefully they will stop now. Because four is an unlucky number in Asian countries.'

'I'd hate to be unlucky,' said Friday sarcastically.

The girls shifted forward in the breakfast line.

'Friday,' said Epstein. He had joined the queue behind them.

'You're still here?' said Friday.

Epstein blushed. 'Dad did teach for the full eight weeks, and my tuition was part of his payment,' he said with a shrug.

'What about next year's tuition?' asked Friday. 'Can your mum afford the fees?'

Epstein smiled. Friday realised she hadn't seen Epstein smile before. 'The Headmaster has offered me an art scholarship if I replace Dad's mural with something less . . . controversial.'

'Good for you,' said Friday.

'But what about the huge painting of Mrs Cannon?' asked Melanie.

'One of the billionaires from the auction has offered to buy it,' said Epstein. 'He's going to pay the full price of the swimming pool. Mrs Cannon is going to decorate the side of his barn in his back paddock.'

'Mrs Cannon will be pleased to be preserved for posterity,' said Melanie.

'But how can he move a mural?' asked Friday.

'The billionaire is going to pay a team of art conservators to remove and transport the entire side of the building,' explained Epstein.

'And the Headmaster agreed to that?' said Friday.

'Apparently, he really doesn't want to look at the mural,' said Epstein. 'I'm not sure what upsets him most – the sight of Mrs Cannon or the reminder that he hired my father.'

The girls collected their breakfasts and went over to their usual table. They were surprised to find Ian already sitting there.

'Morning,' he said, without looking up from the book he was reading.

'Uh,' grunted Friday as she sat down next to him and picked up her fork.

'Oh, isn't that nice,' said Melanie. 'You two have made up. I knew you couldn't stay mad at each other for long. You need each other. No one else can understand half the things you say.'

Friday and Ian continued to ignore Melanie. But the three of them enjoyed the companionable silence. It was nice to have things back the way they should be.

Friday was concentrating so hard on eating the stewed pears in front of her while moving as little of her face as possible, that she didn't notice the dining hall had fallen silent. Ian was still reading his book.

So, amazingly enough, Melanie was the first to notice something was going on.

'Friday,' said Melanie, nudging her friend. 'There is a messenger coming this way with a courier envelope.'

Friday turned round to see a year 8 boy walking towards their table. Friday was just about to reach out to take the envelope when the boy said, 'Wainscott, a courier just delivered this to the front office for you.'

Ian was surprised. He hastily swallowed his mouthful and took the envelope. He looked at it for a moment, but the generic stationery did not reveal any secrets, so he tore it open. A passport, a large wad of cash in a foreign currency and an airline ticket fell onto the table.

'What is that for?' asked Melanie.

A yellow post-it note was stuck to the front of the passport. Ian peeled it off.

'It's a ticket to the Cayman Islands,' said Ian. He read the note aloud, ' "I'm on my feet. Fly out and join me. Love, Dad".'

'When is the ticket for?' asked Friday.

Ian looked up. His eyes locked with Friday's. 'Tonight.'

To find out what happens next, read the sixth
book in the series . . .

FRIDAY BARNES
Danger Ahead

R. A. Spratt

FRIDAY BARNES
Girl Detective

R. A. Spratt

FRIDAY BARNES
Under Suspicion

R. A. Spratt

FRIDAY BARNES
Big Trouble

R. A. Spratt

FRIDAY BARNES
No Rules

R. A. Spratt

FRIDAY BARNES
The Plot Thickens

R. A. Spratt

FRIDAY BARNES
Danger Ahead

R. A. Spratt

FRIDAY BARNES
Bitter Enemies

R. A. Spratt

FRIDAY BARNES
Never Fear

COLLECT THEM ALL!

Meet Nanny Piggins ... a nanny with trotters!

THE RUNAWAY LION

Nanny Piggins

R.A. SPRATT

THE ACCIDENTAL BLAST-OFF

Nanny Piggins

R.A. SPRATT

THE DARING RESCUE

Nanny Piggins

R.A. SPRATT

THE RACE TO POWER

Nanny Piggins

LOVE ROALD DAHL? YOU'LL LOVE THIS!

R.A. SPRATT

COLLECT THEM ALL!

Enter a world of mayhem and adventure with
The Peski Kids!

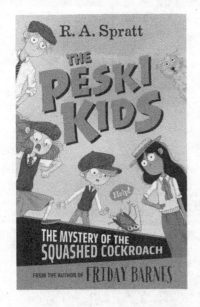

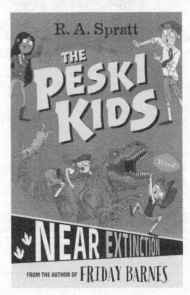

COLLECT THEM ALL!

About the Author

R. A. Spratt is an award-winning author and television writer. She lives in Bowral with her husband and two daughters. Like Friday Barnes, she enjoys wearing a silly hat.

For more information, visit www.raspratt.com